Gliding forward fast, Mark shot out his hands. He laid the right against the side of Shem's head and duplicated the movement on Dub with his left. Before either man could resist, he brought their skulls together. There was a click, like two enormous billiard balls making a cannon, and looking as if they had been boned, the pair collapsed limply on being released.

"Behind you, Mark!" Marlene screamed, pointing to emphasize her meaning.

Pivoting around, the big blonde saw the bartender moving along the counter. Even as the man started to reach for something that was underneath it, Mark's right hand dipped, and the ivory-handled army Colt flowed from his off-side holster.

"Bring them out!" Mark commanded, lining the barrel as the hammer clicked to the rear and his forefinger curled across the trigger . . .

The Hide
and Tallow Men

J. T. Edson

A DELL BOOK

Published by
Dell Publishing
a division of
Bantam Doubleday Dell Publishing Group, Inc.
666 Fifth Avenue
New York, New York 10103

ISBN: 0-440-20862-9

Printed in the United States of America

Published simultaneously in Canada

February 1991

10 9 8 7 6 5 4 3 2 1

RAD

For my new boss,
Diane "Calamity Jane" Lloyd,
and her twelve-foot bullwhip.
Honestly, Di, I will "work hard."

Author's Note

Once again, to enable my regular readers to avoid repetition but to explain things to new chums, I have included the histories of Dusty Fog, Mark Counter, and the Ysabel Kid in the form of appendices.

In Explanation

While complete in itself, this book continues the events re-corded in Set Texas Back on Her Feet. *Points to be remembered from the previous portion of the story are:*

Hearing that Colonel Charles Goodnight was to tell the Ranch Owners' Convention—which was being held at Fort Worth in conjunction with the Tarrant County Fair—of his plan to rebuild the war-ruined economy of Texas by utilizing the vast numbers of long-horned cattle that were roaming the range country, the five owners of the Pilar Hide & Tallow Company had seen a threat to their enormous profits. At that time they and similar organizations were the only market for the cattle; paying, at the highest, four dollars a head, with the calves thrown in free. Goodnight hoped to prove that herds could be driven to the rail-road in Kansas and sold for much higher prices. As he was known as a cattleman of ability and was backed by General Ole Devil Hardin, among others, the partners had believed that he would succeed. If he did, the ranchers would not be compelled to sell to hide and tallow factories for want of a more lucrative market. The benefits that would accrue from Goodnight's plan, even the possible salvation of Texas, had meant nothing to Ber-nard Schweitzer, Pierre de Froissart, Giuseppe Profaci, and Aus-tin and Marlene Viridian. They had decided that they must take action to save their investment.

Austin Viridian had gone to Fort Worth disguised as a cow-hand and accompanied by the factory's floor supervisor, Gus Roxterby, an ex-outlaw with numerous useful contacts. They had had the dual purpose of trying to prevent Goodnight's plan from being accepted even if it should be and to persuade ranch-ers to sign contracts to continue supplying the company with cattle.

Knowing that, under an agreement they had all signed on forming the company, no owner could dispose of his or—in

Marlene's case—her holdings except to the remaining partners, Viridian had taken precautions to protect himself. He had forced them to put into writing and sign that they had known about and concurred with whatever actions he found necessary to carry out his task. Harlow Dolman, a corrupt captain of the state police who had been present, had been a reluctant witness to their signatures. Each of the affected parties had retained a copy of the incriminating document. Viridian had taken two and had warned that they would be used if he should be arrested, to ensure that the others did not try to desert him.

Helped by two of the men Roxterby had hired on their arrival, Viridian had forced a rancher, Paul Dover, to sign a contract. However, his first attempt at preventing Goodnight's views from being circulated had ended in disaster. Learning that Dover had been discussing the matter with what he had described as a "short-growed, blond-haired kid," Viridian had left the rancher in the dark and gone to silence the youngster. While the description had been correct physically, Dover had deliberately failed to mention the "kid's" name. He had proved to be the legendary Captain Dusty Fog.* The omission had cost Dover his life and had resulted in both of Viridian's men being killed. One had been shot by Dusty's amigo, the Ysabel Kid.† Before escaping, Viridian had murdered Dover and the second man to prevent them from being able to identify him.

Finding that he had not been pursued, Viridian had changed into his usual style of clothing and returned to confer with de Froissart, who was to act as the company's official representative at the convention. The hour was late when he had reached the Creole's room. De Froissart had been sleeping with a woman, but had hidden her in the wardrobe before allowing his visitor to enter. She had remained in hiding all the time Viridian had been there and he had pretended to be unaware of her presence.

---

* Details of Dusty Fog's career and special abilities are given in Appendix 1.

† Details of the Ysabel Kid's career and special abilities are given in Appendix 3.

De Froissart had stated that Dusty was not fooled by Viridian's disguise and had given the local peace officers an accurate description of his surviving attacker. Fortunately the investigation had been put in Dolman's hands and, taking out a posse, he had made sure that they did not follow Viridian.

Accepting that it would be unwise and unsafe for him to remain, Viridian had taken his departure. He had been puzzled by the Creole's behavior on his arrival and worried over the way they had discussed the affair with the woman able to overhear every word. Wondering who she was, Viridian had taken advantage of the desk clerk's absence and examined the register. From what he had read and remembered about the visit, he had realized that she was his wife. There was no love between the Viridians, but he had still been furious over her infidelity, mainly because he had felt that she and de Froissart might be laughing at him. Even as he had thought of rushing up and confronting them, using the incident as an excuse to get rid of two partners, a better and safer way had presented itself. Having run into difficulties, Roxterby had arrived to ask de Froissart for advice. Telling the supervisor not to mention they had met, Viridian had bribed him to arrange for the errant pair to be murdered—in such a way that it would seem they were killed in a holdup—on their way home.

Although unaware that she had been found out, Marlene had decided to establish an alibi to "prove" that she had not been in the hotel while her husband was there. Going to a ball given by friends, she had seen Dusty Fog and had decided that he had great potential as a supporter of Goodnight's plan. Later she had met Mark Counter, who was representing his father's R Over C Ranch, and had discovered that he had several qualities that could be turned to her advantage. In addition to having proven himself very skilled in fistfighting and using a gun, he had expressed doubts regarding the feasibility of driving herds to Kansas and appeared to harbor considerable resentment toward Dusty Fog. Realizing that, in Goodnight's absence, Dusty would be a leading protagonist of the plan, Marlene had hoped to induce Mark to kill him. They had fought, but with bare hands, and Mark had accidentally strained his right shoulder. While the injury had not been serious, it had precluded any hope of a showdown with guns.

While disappointed, Marlene had continued her friendship and invited Mark to accompany her when she went home. She had explained to de Froissart and Dolman that other ranchers who had been disinclined to believe that Goodnight's plan would work had also been asked to visit Pilar. It was hoped that they would sign contracts, and being able to show them Mark's signature when they arrived might sway them favorably. However she had not mentioned her real reason for inviting Mark. She intended to spend the week until the other ranchers arrived winning him over and to use him as the means of gaining complete control of the company. As its profits would be reduced when herds began to trail north, she had decided that five partners were excessive to share in them. Not only did she intend to become the sole owner, but she suspected that her partners and Dolman had similar sentiments. Although she had once considered Dolman an ally, she no longer trusted him and felt that the blond youngster would be far more satisfactory and safe.

What Marlene did not know was that Mark was Dusty Fog's amigo. While he had been representing his father, who was in full agreement with Goodnight, he rode for Ole Devil Hardin's OD Connected Ranch.* Before reaching Fort Worth, Dusty and Mark had decided to take advantage of the fact that as yet few people knew of their association. In that way, Mark's support for Goodnight would have a greater effect upon those who were doubtful. Certain remarks made by Marlene on their first meeting had caused Mark not to mention his true status. On hearing of her interest in Mark, Dusty had decided that they would make use of it. From various pieces of evidence, they had come to suspect Viridian was Dover's murderer. So Mark had won Marlene's confidence in the hope of obtaining proof of her husband's guilt. The fight and Mark's "injury"—which had been

---

* Details of Mark Counter's career and special abilities are given in Appendix 2.

"diagnosed" by his uncle, who was a doctor—had been carried out to avoid his having to face Dusty with guns. Having failed to obtain the necessary proof in Fort Worth, Mark had accepted Marlene's offer in the hope that he might find it at Pilar.

The Hide and Tallow Men *commences on the Monday following the end of the Tarrant County Fair.*

1

ARE YOU THREATENING ME?

As Austin Viridian strolled out of the main entrance to the Pilar Hide & Tallow Company's factory, there was nothing about him to suggest that he believed his wife would be dead before sundown.

Tall, broad-shouldered, and in his late thirties, Viridian had close-cropped brown hair that was receding from coarse, irregular features. Reddened and puffy from much good living, they had surly lines, which warned of an ill-tempered nature. Clad in a white "planter's" hat, black broadcloth coat, fancy vest, white silk shirt, and black cravat of the same material, yellowish-brown Nankeen trousers, and black Hersome gaiter boots, he bore an ivory-handled Remington New Model Police revolver in the cross-draw holster on the left side of his gunbelt. It was anything but a decoration. Although there was a pronounced thickening at his waist, he still looked strong and powerful.

Until a few minutes earlier, clad in just his vest and trousers, he had been killing the cattle that the corral crew—under their supervisor, Stack Leathers—had sent up the chute that led into the factory. As one of the five partners who owned the company, there had been no real need for him to work as a slaughterman. He did so when the mood took him because he enjoyed carrying out the task and derived considerable pleasure from watching a large, powerful creature tumble dead as a result of his expert wielding of a poleax. It was his frequently made boast that he could down a longhorn—be it a yearling, steer, full-grown cow, or prime bull, the factory took and used them all regardless of age or sex—faster and more neatly than any man on the company's payroll.

As always when carrying out his self-appointed task, Viridian had found himself experiencing a sensation of sexual stimulation. So, having told one of the Negro factory hands to continue the slaughtering, he had dressed and set off to find female company with whom he could satisfy the feeling. His wife had been attending the Tarrant County Fair and, if all went as planned, would not be returning alive. Not that he had considered her as the means of gratifying his lust. Giuseppe Profaci had left Pilar the previous Friday on a business trip. So Viridian hoped to find his Italian partner's wife in an accommodating frame of mind. Gianna had been on two occasions, but they had failed as yet to make the most of her husband and his wife's absence.

Viridian felt certain that an assignation could be accomplished with little danger of them being caught in the act. Every Monday morning Gianna could be found doing the family's laundry—herself, not the servants, just like Momma back in the Old Country, Profaci had often explained with pride—in the stream that flowed through the woodland to the rear of hers and the Viridians' homes. He wondered if he should give Gianna a hint of his hopes regarding Marlene and decided to do so only if she continued to display the reluctance to yield to his wishes that had been in evidence since Profaci's departure.

Standing just inside the open double doors, Gus Roxterby watched his employer leaving. The floor supervisor was a tall, lanky, unhappy-looking man with a broken nose and a partially bald head. As always, his well-worn range clothes had acquired numerous splashes of blood. Slanting down from his left hip, a gunbelt supported a Colt 1860 army revolver—the barrel of which had been cut down to four inches and the rammer adjusted accordingly—in a tied-down, contoured holster. Despite his lugubrious appearance, he was reasonably fast with the gun and used it if the slaughterman should fail to make a clean kill.

Taking his opportunity while Viridian had been dressing, Roxterby had brought the conversation around to the task he had been given in Fort Worth. He had assured his employer that only the leader of the gang he had hired would know their real purpose in committing the holdup. With it carried out, the outlaw would come to Frog Creek—about a mile from Pilar—on Wednesday night to collect the balance of his payment. On Viridian querying the advisability of allowing the man to come so close to the town, Roxterby had replied that it would be lead and not gold he would receive on his arrival.

However, despite Roxterby having mentioned that he had been compelled to advance the outlaw a hundred and fifty dollars—the actual amount had only been a hundred—the hide and tallow man had not been receptive to a hint that he would like the money that had been promised for making the arrangements. To do the supervisor justice, he could appreciate his employer's reluctance to making the payment at that time. If their positions had been reversed, he most certainly would not have handed over the five hundred dollars until he was sure that it had been earned. So he could hardly blame Viridian for refusing. The trouble was that Roxterby also knew that he would have tried to find some way of paying the promised sum. Doubting that Viridian would prove any more honorable, he saw danger to himself. From now on, if Widge carried out his instructions, he might have to step warily if he wanted to stay alive.

Without realizing that his floor supervisor was watching him, or guessing at the thoughts that were running through Roxterby's head, Viridian glanced to his right. He did not expect to find the small office annex occupied. Concentrating upon their second business interests in Pilar, his male partners left him to run the factory. So the office was used only for

general administrative purposes. All of the company's business
deals were carried out in the back room of Schweitzer's General Store. Previously, having felt that it belittled his abilities,
Viridian had disapproved of the system. He was now compelled
to admit that it had certain advantages.

A faint grin creased the hide and tallow man's face as he
gazed at the office. In the small safe, concealed among the unimportant papers, which were usually all that it held, were
three items that his wife, partners, or Harlow Dolman would be
very pleased to see destroyed. He did not doubt that the two
copies of the statement they had all signed were responsible for
his safe return from Fort Worth. Without them, Dolman would
have hunted him down and, having killed him, buried him to
prevent his body being identified.

The third document was the contract that Viridian had compelled Paul Dover to sign. Although he had realized that it was
even more incriminating than the statements, he could not
bring himself to destroy it. He hoped that he might still be able
to make the rancher's widow honor it at a later date. Retaining
it might be dangerous, but he felt sure that nobody would suspect him of using such an obvious hiding place.

Hearing the sound of hooves approaching, Viridian turned
his gaze from the office. What he saw drove all thoughts of the
safe from his head. Three riders had turned from the stagecoach trail and were coming along the track that connected it
to the factory. Clad in sombreros and filthy charro clothing,
well-armed, they were Mexicans.

Studying the trio, Viridian felt worried. He could identify
only one of them, Juan Ribagorza's *segundo,* who went by the
name Gomez. While the *segundo*'s lack of stature, straggling
mustache, and apologetic manner made him seem harmless and
even comical, Viridian knew him to be as unpredictably savage
as a stick-teased diamondback rattlesnake. He was probably far
more dangerous than either of his larger, heavier companions.
Which did not imply that they would be harmless. Individually
or as a group, they were real bad *hombres.* Ribagorza did not
hire any other kind of men.

There was, Viridian tried to tell himself, no reason why he should feel uneasy over the trio's arrival. Although Ribagorza did not own a ranch, he had frequently delivered herds of cattle for sale to the company, for which he had received only one dollar a head, but without being asked embarrassing questions about how the longhorns—invariably bearing a variety of brands—had come into his possession. None of his hard-case crew had ever caused any trouble. Being aware of how useful the lack of questioning was, Ribagorza had always ensured that the visits went off peacefully. Yet Viridian had always sensed that Gomez nursed a bitter hatred toward white people and was only held in check by his employer.

Instead of riding right up to the factory and dismounting, the three men acted in an unusual manner. They swung their horses in a half circle, to halt facing away from the building. Then, leaving the one-piece reins draped over the huge horns of their single-cinched saddles, they swung to the ground. With Gomez in the center, they walked toward Viridian. All the time their eyes were darting about them in a wary fashion.

Standing apparently relaxed, but with his right hand's thumb hooked just to the left of the gunbelt's buckle, Viridian examined his visitors with considerable interest and growing concern. Even when Ribagorza had been present, he had never felt completely at ease with Gomez. To add to his perturbation, there was something sinister in the way the trio was slouching forward. They looked like men who were expecting trouble.

Wondering what had brought the trio to the factory, for they had never come except when accompanying Ribagorza and a herd of cattle, Viridian noticed that there was a partly healed weal running across Gomez's left cheek. It looked like the kind of injury that would be caused by a blow from a riding quirt.

"*Saludos, Señor* Viridian," Gomez greeted, coming to a halt about two yards away from the burly man. As if sensing that the ridge of reddened flesh had attracted the other's notice, he raised his left hand toward it. Without completing the gesture or referring to the injury, he darted a glance at the open double doors of the factory and continued in Spanish, "My *patrón* sent me to speak with you."

"You'll have to talk English, I don't savvy Mex," Viridian answered, confident that the other did not know he was lying. He had always conducted all his business with Ribagorza in his own native tongue, although reasonably fluent in Spanish.

"My *patrón* said I should come and see you, *señor,*" Gomez obliged in broken but understandable English.

"What about?" Viridian asked, genuinely puzzled.

At no time had Ribagorza ever allowed even his *segundo* to discuss business with the owners of the factory. Nor had he, being aware of Gomez's antipathy toward white men, allowed the other to precede him on a visit.

"He said I should tell you he's got maybe five hundred head of cattle down the river a ways," Gomez replied.

"I reckon we might be able to use them," Viridian said in a disinterested manner and concealing his elation. With the threat of many ranchers driving herds to Kansas, he believed that it would be advisable to obtain as many cattle as possible.

"We thought you might, *señor,*" Gomez said, in a mocking tone.

"Why'd Ribagorza send you?" Viridian demanded, scowling. "He's never needed to let us know he's coming."

"No, *señor,*" Gomez admitted with a sly grin. "But things aren't like they was before anymore, are they?"

"What might *that* mean?" Viridian growled, although he could guess what was coming.

"People are saying that cattle taken to Kansas're going to be worth a lot of money, *señor,*" Gomez explained in the whining voice and exhibiting the pathetic attitude that made him appear to be a nervous and frightened little man.

"If they can be got there," Viridian countered.

"Colonel Goodnight says they can."

"That doesn't make it so. And, anyways, even if you got them there, you'd have to prove how you got hold of 'em. You know what I mean?"

"Just about, *señor,*" Gomez admitted.

"Ribagorza'll know, when you tell him," Viridian declared. "So what's on his mind, huh?"

"These cattle, *señor*. We went to a lot of trouble to get them—"

"No more than any other time," Viridian interrupted unsympathetically.

"And, with them being so valuable," Gomez continued as if the other had not spoken, "my *patrón* says they're worth six dollars a head."

"*Six* dollars a head?" Viridian repeated. That was two dollars higher than the legitimate price, and the Mexicans, bringing in stolen cattle, had never received more than a dollar for each animal they had delivered. "If this's Ribagorza's idea of a joke—"

"Is no joke, *señor*," Gomez put in, looking and acting at his most meek and mild. Which, as Viridian was all too aware, meant that he was more dangerous than ever. He had behaved like that just before killing one of his companions on a previous visit. "My *patrón* says he wants six dollars a head. And you've got to send him two hundred dollars to show you'll have the herd when he gets it here."

Cold rage boiled inside Viridian as he listened to the small Mexican. He knew that if he yielded to such a demand, he would be leaving the company wide open for further abuses. Any sign of weakness would be exploited in full by Ribagorza.

"So that's what he says, huh?" Viridian said, gritting his teeth.

"That's just what he says, *señor*," Gomez confirmed. "So, if you'll give me the money—"

"I'll give you nothing!" Viridian snarled furiously, his normal dislike for Mexicans combining with indignation at the request to make him ignore the menacing attitudes of the men flanking Gomez. "You get the hell back and tell him this from me. He'll get the same price we've always paid him and not a thin red cent more. And he'll get the money when the cattle are in the corrals, not before. If he doesn't like it, he can try to sell them to somebody else."

"If I tell him that, *señor,*" Gomez almost whined, "he's going to be very angry. He's got a lot of men with him. Maybe it's better you give me the two hundred dollars, so I can take it to him and he don't get angry at you."

"Are you threatening me?" Viridian challenged.

"Who me, *señor*?" Gomez yelped. "I don't threaten nobody. All I can say is my *patrón*'s not going to be happy if a *gringo* sends him a message like that. He'll be very angry at you, *señor.*"

"I'll take my chance on it!" Viridian stated.

"Maybe if you gave me just one hundred dollars—" Gomez began hopefully.

"I wouldn't give you a hundred wooden nickels!" Viridian assured him. "So you can go and tell him what I said."

"Well, I tried," the little Mexican said with a sigh, sounding genuinely distressed. "We'll go and tell our *patrón* what you said. I only hope you don't be sorry."

"I'll take my chance on it," Viridian replied coldly. "Just don't *you* do anything you'll be sorry for."

"Who me, *señor*?" Gomez answered. "As if I would." Then he addressed his companions in their native tongue. "We don't get the money. Do what I told you."

Nodding in an apologetically amiable fashion, as if he regretted having to deliver such a message, the *segundo* swung on his heel toward the waiting horses. His two men also turned and they started to walk away.

Scowling, Viridian watched them go. He was puzzled by the incident. Knowing him, Ribagorza ought to have had better sense than to expect that he would yield to such a demand. While he was pondering the matter, a snort from one of the horses drew his gaze to where they were standing with their rumps turned in his direction.

Why had the trio left their mounts in such a position?

Could it be because they had believed that they might need to take a hurried departure?

If so—

"*Ahora!*" snapped the small *segundo*, stabbing his right hand to its gun.

Instantly, showing that they had been waiting for Gomez to say, "Now!" the other two Mexicans joined him in pivoting to face Viridian, with their revolvers beginning to lift from the holsters. They discovered that their surprise attack had not been an unqualified success.

Already diving sideways and down to his left, the burly hide and tallow man was snatching his Remington from its cross-draw holster. For all his size, he was moving very fast.

Realization of his peril had added speed to Viridian's movements as he, too, had heard and translated Gomez's command. Taken with what he had just begun to think, it had given him enough of a warning to set off his defensive reflexes. For all that, he knew that he was in bad, even desperate, trouble. Although his actions had been unexpected by his assailants and despite the fact that he would be the first man holding a gun, he would not be able to deal with the three of them swiftly enough to save his own life. He would certainly down Gomez and might get one more, but the other was sure to kill him.

Oblivious of the impact as his body landed on the ground, Viridian concentrated on lining his weapon. He was determined on two things: to sell his life dearly and to make sure that he took Gomez with him. With the Remington pointed to his satisfaction, while the little man was still in the process of throwing down on him, he squeezed the trigger. Flying upward at an angle, the .36-caliber bullet entered beneath the small Mexican's chin. Driving on, to pass through the roof of his mouth and his brain, it burst from the top of his skull and caused his sombrero to jerk as it emerged out of the crown. Killed instantly, Gomez allowed his revolver to slip from his fingers. It went off, but the bullet did no more than drill into the ground a couple of feet ahead of Viridian.

Any satisfaction that Viridian might have felt at having settled Gomez's hash was swamped by the knowledge of how he was himself in imminent danger of getting shot by his victim's companions.

What the hide and tallow man did not realize was that help was available for him.

Gus Roxterby had been on the point of returning to his work when he had seen the Mexicans approaching. Curiosity had impelled him to watch and listen to what was happening; but prudence had dictated that he remain out of sight so as to prevent Viridian from discovering that he was not attending to his duties. When he had heard the trend the conversation was taking, he had suspected that it might lead to trouble. So he was not sorry that he had taken the precaution of remaining concealed behind the edge of the door. Although the Mexicans had looked in his direction, he had escaped detection as he kept them under observation. Sharing his employer's mistrust of Gomez, he had drawn and cocked his Colt. The sound of the action being brought to full cock had been drowned by the various noises that were coming from behind him.

Money, not loyalty, was Roxterby's reason for being willing to protect Viridian. If he should be killed and Widge was successful in carrying out the two murders, the floor supervisor would have no way of collecting the payment he had been promised.

Nor was Roxterby the only person who had taken an interest in the arrival of the Mexicans. Having come into contact with Gomez on previous visits, the corral supervisor, Stack Leathers, had never trusted him and knew that he had a hatred of gringos that was only held in check by Ribagorza's presence. Seeing that the *segundo* was coming without the restraining influence of his *patrón,* Leathers had decided to keep an unsuspected eye on him. So, collecting the Spencer carbine from the boot of his horse's saddle, he had moved unnoticed to the end of the building. Staying out of sight, he had listened to what was being said and had just looked out when Gomez's party launched their attack.

Shock twisted at the faces of the two burly Mexicans as they realized that their leader's plan had gone completely wrong. Not only had they failed to take the hide and tallow man by surprise, but he had support in defending himself. A tall, skinny gringo holding a revolver appeared at the main entrance to the factory. Swinging a carbine into the firing position, a medium-sized, well-built, bearded man in range clothing stepped into view around the northern end of the building.

Supporting his right hand by cupping the left under it, Roxterby took swift aim along the shortened barrel of his Colt. Unfortunately he selected the same target as Leathers. Carbine and revolver crashed at almost the same instant. Struck in the breast and the head by the bullets, the man was pitched sideways. Spinning helplessly, he collided with Gomez's crumpling body, and they fell together.

Being unaware of the two supervisors' intervention, Viridian was trying to select the more dangerous of his remaining assailants. Both appeared to be equally as fast and deadly. Thumbing back the hammer of his Remington, he became aware that they had looked away from him and were displaying considerable consternation. Even as he wondered what had brought this about, he learned the answer. The deep roar of a heavy revolver and the sharper detonation of a carbine sounded from behind him, the bullets finding their billets in the man on the right.

There was no time for the hide and tallow man to feel gratitude or relief. While the surviving Mexican was flustered by the unexpected turn of events, he held a weapon and was still anything but harmless. All that was saving Viridian was the man's irresolution. Confronted by three enemies, he wavered uncertainly as he tried to work out which of them posed the greatest threat to him. Before he could reach a decision, Viridian had swung the Remington into alignment. It spat and kicked, throwing its load into the Mexican's right breast. Reeling back a couple of steps, the man neither fell nor dropped his gun.

Seeing that their employer had failed to disable his last attacker, Roxterby and Leathers devoted their respective attentions to him. Working the carbine's combined trigger guard-loading lever, Leathers ejected the spent cartridge case and replenished the chamber with a live bullet from the seven-shot magazine tube in the butt. However, with that done, he still had to cock the big side-hammer manually. So Roxterby fired first, but missed. The bullet flew by its intended mark, to plow into the rump of Gomez's mount. Down went the stricken animal, kicking and squealing. Already made restless by the shooting, the other two horses bolted as its agony-filled screams assailed their ears. Snorting in alarm, they fled toward the stagecoach trail.

Snarling out curses that were rendered almost incoherent by rage and pain, the Mexican heard the horses running away. He knew that he could not hope to escape, so he tried to aim at Viridian. Even as he was starting to squeeze the trigger, the .52-caliber bullet from Leathers's Spencer carbine slammed into his right temple and tore away half his face as it came out the other side.

Having recocked the Remington, Viridian was on the point of firing. He refrained from doing so as he saw the result of Leathers's shot. Instead he started to rise. Glaring at the three Mexicans, he ignored the shouts that were raised at the corral and inside the factory. Not until he was sure that he had nothing further to fear from his attackers did he lower the weapon and turn around. Holstering his Colt, Roxterby was approaching. Glaring about him, in much the same manner as a long-horned bull that smelled blood, Viridian noticed that men were appearing at the door of the building and running from the corral.

Allowing the smoke carbine to sink from its firing position, Leathers glanced at his employer. Then he swung his gaze to the fleeing horses and a low curse burst from his lips. Hearing some of the men running from the corral, he swung around.

"Lem, Dink!" Leathers said, pointing after the departing animals with his left hand. "Get after them hosses. Kill 'em if you have to, but don't let 'em get away."

"Sure thing, Massa Leathers," replied the tallest of the Negroes and, accompanied by the other man who had been named, he ran to where the horses used for controlling the cattle were tethered to the corral.

Having attended to what he regarded as a matter of the greatest importance, the corral supervisor went to join Viridian and Roxterby. They were looking at him in a puzzled manner, clearly wondering why he had given such an order.

"Ribagorza's not going to take it kind, us killing them three," Leathers warned in his lazy Texas drawl. "So we don't want their hosses getting back to him."

Listening to the reason for the corral supervisor's actions, neither Viridian nor Roxterby needed any further explanation. Range-bred horses possessed an uncanny ability to find their way back to their homes, or to rejoin their companions in the remuda when on the move. So the Mexicans' mounts had to be prevented from returning to Ribagorza. The old saying "A man afoot is no man at all" was very true anywhere west of the Mississippi River. Particularly in Texas, where a horse went far beyond being a mere means of getting from one place to another and was a vital necessity for survival, the sight of one returning with an empty saddle was cause for alarm.

Looking at Leathers, Viridian nodded with approval. Dressed in worn, but fairly clean, range clothing, with a tinge of gray in his brown hair and beard, Leathers had none of Roxterby's miserable, hangdog look. Tough and capable, he was competent if not exceptional in the use of the wooden-handled Colt 1860 army revolver that rode butt forward in the contoured holster tied to his right thigh.

"He'll know for sure something's wrong when Gomez don't come back, anyways." Roxterby protested, not caring for his employer displaying approbation toward Leathers.

"Likely," the corral supervisor conceded. "Only I don't see any sense in letting him find out about it any sooner than he has to."

While agreeing with Leathers, Viridian found a fresh source of annoyance as he looked at the Negroes. Relief over his narrow escape had done little to improve his temper. In addition to being furious over Ribagorza's effrontery and Gomez's treacherous attack, he realized that the incident might have an adverse effect upon his plans for spending a pleasant period of dalliance with Gianna Profaci. He would be delayed to such an extent that, even if she was still in the woods, there would be little time for him to fully satisfy his lust. What was more, Leathers had raised a point that did not improve matters.

"Get the hell back to your work!" Viridian bellowed, venting his anger upon the colored employees. "There's nothing for you to see or do out here!"

"Where do you reckon Ribagorza's at, boss?" Leathers inquired, as the Negroes returned to their work chattering excitedly among themselves.

"Gomez reckoned he had his herd down the river," Viridian answered. "Which doesn't tell us much."

"Nope," Leathers agreed. "But, way things've turned out, we'd best find out for sure just how far off he is and what he's fixing to do."

"You'd best go and see if you can find him," Viridian suggested, knowing that the corral supervisor was capable of carrying out the task. He was tougher, smarter, and faster with a gun than Roxterby, if possessing less useful contacts. "Don't let them know you're around, and come back as soon as you're sure he's headed this way."

"I'll 'tend to it," Leathers promised.

"Have some of the men load the bodies onto a wagon and move that horse," Viridian told Roxterby and decided that he should make a gesture to show the supervisors his gratitude. "You two can share their gear between you. I'll tell Josh Hubric that I said you could."

"We'll do the splitting when I get back, Gus," Leathers stated, knowing that the town constable would not refuse Viridian's orders. "All of it, mind. No picking and choosing after I'm gone."

"Sure, Stack," Roxterby replied. Sharing his employer's opinion regarding Leathers's ability with a gun, he hid the resentment he was feeling at the other's words. "You can count on me to play square with you."

"I reckon I can," Leathers said dryly. "See you when I get back."

"I'll send some men out from town to help you guard the

factory," Viridian remarked to the floor supervisor as Leathers walked away. "Stay on until I send for you."

"Do you reckon Ribagorza'll be here soon, boss?" Roxterby asked, realizing that, with Viridian's and Leathers's departure, he would be the only white man on the premises.

"If he is, Leathers will let you know in good time," Viridian answered, having devoted some thought to the matter and reached certain conclusions. "I'll get as many men as I can out to you. When they come, set them out ready to guard the factory."

"Sure, boss," Roxterby muttered, and his whole attitude showed how serious and dangerous he considered the situation to be.

2

NONE OF US DARE
BETRAY HIM

Marlene Viridian did not usually indulge in romantic fantasies; she was far too hardheaded and calculating for that. Yet as she considered her present situation, she could not help thinking that she was not unlike a princess of old, with no less than three knights-errant competing for her favors. Sitting at the small folding table, which Pierre de Froissart's Negro valet had set up, she wondered if the pleasant and peaceful nature of her surroundings had conjured up such a foolish notion.

Having left Fort Worth on Sunday morning, traveling south along the stagecoach trail and spending the night at a way station, Marlene's party had resumed their journey shortly after dawn on Monday. Although she and the Creole were riding in the Pilar Hide & Tallow Company's private Abbot & Downing "celerity coach," they had not attempted to make the best speed its six-horse team was capable of producing. Noon had found them passing through wooded country and approaching a suitable location for them to halt and take lunch.

Receiving his orders, the Negro driver had guided his team off the trail and stopped close to the banks of a small, crystal-clear stream. There was a clearing at that point, although it did not extend to the right side of the trail. While the horses were being unhitched, the valet had unpacked the folding table, four chairs, and a large picnic hamper from the coach's boat.

By the stream the driver was still attending to the needs of the team. Not far away a big chestnut gelding and an even larger, finer bloodbay stallion were hobbled and grazing. Two saddles—a United States Army "officer's pattern" McClellan and a low-horner, double-girthed* Texas range rig—lay on their sides behind the coach, where they would not be in the way of the driver or the valet.

Although Marlene studied two of her "champions," the third was not in evidence. Soon after the party had halted, a turkey had started to call from the thick woodland on the right of the trail. Being very partial to roast turkey, Marlene had suggested that one of her escort try to shoot the bird. Mark Counter had immediately offered his services and had stated that the hunt should be a one-man affair. Neither de Froissart nor Dolman had argued on that point. So, having unsaddled his bloodbay stallion, Mark had taken his rifle and disappeared into the dense undergrowth.

Sitting at Marlene's right, between her and the trail, de Froissart was about medium height and in his late forties; which made him older and smaller than either of his rivals. Bareheaded, his grayish hair made his handsome features more distinguished. He wore a gray coat, frilly-bosomed white shirt with a black silk cravat, skintight fawn riding breeches, and black riding boots. Due to the warmth of the day, he had left off his fancy vest and, with it, the pair of Remington Double Derringers that always occupied its pockets. However, he was not entirely unarmed, for his sword-cane was leaning on the right side of his chair.

Dolman had taken the place on the other side of Marlene and nearest to the coach. There was nothing in his appearance to suggest that he held rank as a captain in the state police. Rather he looked like a rich, elegant, somewhat arrogant young

---

* Due to its Mexican connotations, few Texans used the word *cinch*.

eastern dandy. The black Burnside campaign hat that he had
hung on the back of his chair was an officer's model, with its
brim down and minus any kind of insignia. He wore a waist-
long brown leather jacket, gray shirt, gaily colored bandanna,
tight-legged brown riding breeches and hessian boots. All the
garments were of excellent cut and quality. They set off his tall,
athletically slender physique, black curly hair, and handsome,
if sardonic, features to their best advantage.

Dolman's gunbelt carried a rosewood-handled Colt 1861
navy belt pistol—a revolver despite its name—in a split-
fronted, spring-retention holster of a type known as a "clamshell." The drop of the holster was attached to the belt by a
metal swivel stud, and the tip hung free with no means of secur-
ing it to the right thigh. All of the weapon's trigger guard was
left exposed. That had been done to allow his right forefinger to
pass through and make contact with a flat switch concealed on
the rear of the holster. On the switch being pressed, the front of
the rig hinged open and liberated the revolver.

In skilled hands a "clamshell" holster was very fast. Dolman
had always believed himself to be exceptionally competent in its
use.

That the two men should have an interest in Marlene was
understandable. In addition to being very attractive and, under
the right conditions, forthcoming, she was well-bred, wealthy—
and a full partner in the Pilar Hide & Tallow Company. Knowing her feelings with regard to her husband, each of them was
equally aware of how useful she could be to the fulfillment of
his plans for the future.

In her middle thirties Marlene was very beautiful. There was,
however, an imperious, haughty look to her features that suggested she could be strong-willed and not a little arrogant. Her
brunette hair was drawn into a bun and held by a net, being
topped by a Baden hat the front of which was decorated by an
ibis plume. A gray Balmoral traveling costume emphasized her
Junoesque figure in a manner that was attractive and yet socially acceptable. Under it lay rich, full curves which de Froissart and Dolman had cause to know very well.

Looking across the table, the Creole studied Dolman with a speculative gaze. De Froissart suspected that the captain had been as close as he had to Marlene and for the same reason. Being a full partner, the woman would be invaluable to anybody who wished to gain control of the company. That was de Froissart's intention. So he did not relish the thought of having a rival as unscrupulous as Dolman had proved himself to be on more than one occasion. However, thinking about the events of the last few days and, in particular, the previous evening, de Froissart was inclined to believe that Dolman was no longer the greatest threat to his interest in Marlene.

Much the same thoughts were running through Dolman's head. Although he had been of much use to the hide and tallow men, he had no part in the ownership of the company. That had been a situation that he intended to change with Marlene's help, but he sensed that his position with her was endangered by Mark Counter. He did not care for the idea at all, but last night had shown him that changing it might be far from easy.

Always a realist, Dolman had quickly realized that there was no real future for him in the state police. Even though he held high rank, it offered him little profit. What was more, once the people of Texas regained the franchise they had lost through their support of the South during the War Between the States, Governor Davis's corrupt Reconstruction Administration would be swept out of office. One of the first official acts by whoever replaced Davis would be to disband the much-hated state police and reinstate the Texas Rangers. Before that could happen, Dolman wanted to control an established and lucrative business. The Pilar Hide & Tallow Company had struck him as being ideally suited to his needs.

On learning that Marlene had invited Mark Counter to accompany her, Dolman had stated that he, too, would go along. The journey had not been a success for him so far. Every attempt he had made to be alone with the woman had been thwarted by one of his rivals, or—more significantly—by Marlene herself. Deciding that the blond giant, with his advantages of youth and superior physical attraction, was the greater threat, Dolman concluded that he must try to make his peace with the Creole.

"Counter's shoulder got better soon," Dolman remarked, selecting a subject that he felt sure would divert de Froissart's thoughts from his own presence.

"I noticed that," the Creole admitted, glancing covertly at Marlene to try to discover if their words were having any effect. "His uncle must be a good doctor to have cured him just in time for him to leave Fort Worth."

While the woman continued to stare fixedly ahead, to where the trail disappeared around the foot of the wooded slope up which the man they were discussing had gone in search of the turkey, de Froissart noticed that her lips had tightened. Apparently she did not care for the trend of the conversation.

"You know, Pierre," Dolman said, also having noticed Marlene's signs of disapproval. "Dusty Fog was lucky that Counter hurt his shoulder when they fought. If it hadn't happened, they might have had a showdown with guns."

"They might," de Froissart agreed. "Counter's real fast too."

Try as he might, the Creole could not prevent just a hint of malicious delight from creeping into his voice as he spoke the last sentence. What was more, he saw that the barb had gone home.

"Yes," the captain said, gritting his teeth and scowling.

"Of course," de Froissart went on, having no desire to antagonize the other man as long as Mark Counter was around and in Marlene's favor, "drawing and shooting at a barrel doesn't prove anything. There's no comparison between that and facing a man in a real gunfight."

At Marlene's instigation the previous night, Dolman and the big blonde had competed against each other in a gun-handling contest behind the way station. Although the captain had been confident he could win, he found that—despite the advantage that he had believed the "clamshell" holster would give him— Mark was faster and more accurate.

Listening to the Creole's second comment, Dolman felt mollified. De Froissart had put his own sentiments into words.

After the contest he had tried to console himself with the thought that the result had little or no practical meaning. It would have been a different matter if they had been confronting each other with serious intentions, instead of standing side by side and firing on a signal at two empty wine barrels. As the Creole had said, there was no similarity between that and taking part in a real shoot-out.

"They do say that Fog's faced his man in a gunfight more than once," Dolman answered. "And walked away from them. I wonder how many men Counter's put down?"

Realizing that the men were studying her surreptitiously, Marlene attempted to prevent her feelings from showing. For all that, she felt called upon to try to change the line being taken by the men. It would not do for them to become united in their efforts to dispose of the young Texan. She believed that she could divert their thoughts from him. The matter she would raise was of the greatest interest to both men. It was also something to which she had devoted considerable thought, and she wondered whether either of them had drawn any conclusions on it.

"I wonder what Austin did with his copies of that damned statement he had us all sign?" Marlene inquired, and was gratified by the change that came over her companions. "I won't feel easy in my mind until I've seen every last one of them destroyed."

"Or me," Dolman admitted, knowing that not even his considerable political influence could help him evade the consequences if the incriminating documents should fall into the wrong hands.

"We should never have signed them in the first place!" de Froissart said, putting aside his thoughts of Mark Counter on having been reminded of what might develop into an infinitely more dangerous and serious matter. "From the way Austin talked, anybody would have thought that he couldn't trust us."

That was, Marlene told herself, the kind of foolish and pointless remark that she had come to expect from the Creole. While she could appreciate the necessity of keeping up appearances

before business acquaintances, it was sheer hypocrisy for him to
pretend to Dolman and herself that the partners were good
friends or trusted each other.

"As if he couldn't," Dolman sneered, clearly sharing the
woman's unspoken thoughts on the other man's comment.
"But he was right about one thing, even though he didn't come
straight out and say it."

"What's that?" de Froissart wanted to know, scowling as he
studied the Captain's derisive expression.

"As long as he's got them," Dolman explained, "none of us
dare betray him."

"None of *us* intended to betray him," the Creole declared
indignantly, and his dislike for the Captain began to return.

"I never thought you had," Dolman countered, adopting a
placating manner as his glance strayed to the blond giant's
bloodbay stallion. "But you all agreed to sign the damned
things and that I was a witness."

"That was Austin's idea, not mine," de Froissart protested,
also remembering Mark and wanting to keep on reasonably
friendly terms with his less dangerous rival.

"I couldn't see what harm it would do at the time," Dolman
admitted, accepting what amounted to an olive branch. "The
trouble is that they make all of us"—he flickered a glance at
Marlene to make sure that she knew she was included—"acces-
sories to Paul Dover's murder."

"If we could get hold of his copies, we could destroy them
and our own," de Froissart remarked, and made a gesture toward his jacket's left breast. "But I don't intend to get rid of
mine while anybody else has a copy."

"Neither do I," Dolman admitted. Having noticed the un-
completed motion, he guessed that, like himself, the Creole had
not taken the chance of letting his copy out of his possession
and was carrying it with him. To prevent the other from realizing what he suspected, he went on, "Do you have any idea of
what Austin did with his copy, Marlene?"

"No," the woman confessed, drawing similar conclusions

from de Froissart's action, "I can't think of anybody he'd trust to hold them for him."

"How about you, Pierre?" Dolman inquired.

"I can't bring anybody to mind," the Creole replied, hoping that neither of his companions guessed that he was carrying his statement. "Would he have sent them to Boston, do you think?"

"It's not likely," Dolman objected. "They were for his protection if he should be arrested in Fort Worth. If he'd needed them, they'd have to be much closer than that."

Marlene had turned her gaze to the wooded slope, searching for Mark. There had not been any shooting, which suggested that he was still trying to kill the turkey for her. That was all to the good. She wanted to gather as much information as possible before his return caused the conversation to be brought to an end.

"I'm inclined to agree with Harlow," Marlene said. "He would need to have them readily available in case things went wrong. But he wouldn't chance having them with him. Would you, Harlow?"

"No," Dolman replied, and sounded so convincing that the other two believed him.

"Or me," de Froissart went on, just a shade too quickly and without realizing that he had fallen into Marlene's trap. "I left mine in the safe at the New Orleans."

"Mine's hidden at home," Marlene remarked, feeling certain that she had guessed correctly about the Creole. Unlike Dolman, who was sure to have taken precautions for preventing it falling into the wrong hands, de Froissart was carrying his copy and had not left it at his saloon in Pilar. "But I can't think who Austin would trust with them."

While the other two were talking, Dolman stared at the tablecloth. Like Marlene, he could not think of anybody who Viridian would trust sufficiently to hold the documents that were his protection. Probably he had been carrying them all the time. Annoyance welled through the Captain at the thought. If it was true, he could have hunted down and killed Viridian instead of leading the posse in the wrong direction. However it was too late to rectify the miscalculation. What mattered was to lay hands on them.

Where would Viridian have put them on his return from Fort Worth?

Would he have hidden them in his home?

That was unlikely. Knowing he could not trust his wife, he would want a safer place than that.

Safe! Dolman stirred slightly as he thought of another meaning for the word.

There was a safe in the office at the factory!

Of all the partners, Viridian alone used the office as a place of work.

For a moment Dolman was tempted to ignore the safe as a possibility. It seemed to be too obvious a hiding place. Yet Viridian might have selected it for just that reason, counting on anybody who was trying to steal the statements disregarding it as being too obvious.

Although Dolman decided that the office's safe would be worth investigating and believed that he could find the means to do so, he had no intention of mentioning it to de Froissart or Marlene. The possession of the statements would be too valuable an asset to share, even with the woman he was prepared to marry—after having disposed of her present husband—so as to pave the way for him to gain control of the company.

Before the discussion could be taken any farther, half a dozen riders came slowly around the bend in the trail. Dirty, unshaven, dressed in an indiscriminate mixture of cheap range clothing and items of military uniforms, they were not imposing specimens despite the low-hanging revolvers each of them was sporting. On seeing the trio seated at the table, they brought their horses to a halt. Then one of them, a lanky beanpole with a drooping mustache, addressed the others quietly.

Marlene, de Froissart, and Dolman had been too engrossed in their conversation to have heard the sound of the horses' hooves. Stopping their conversation, they looked at the riders.

Although they could not hear what was being said, they guessed that they were the subject of the comments.

"It could be them, boys," the lanky man remarked. "Fancy coach, two niggers. The woman and the short feller fits the descriptions I was given."

"Hell, Widge," protested one of the others. "You allowed ther'd only be the one white feller along."

"So they must've asked the dude to come along." The lanky man sniffed. "From the looks of him, he won't make things no harder. Let's ride in shooting and make sure's he don't, huh?"

"Like hell!" growled the protestor. "We're here to take that money's you reckon they're toting. I ain't standing for no killing, 'less there's no other way."

"Or me," a third man declared. "Killing means hanging, for sure."

Going by the mutters of agreement, Widge decided that the sentiment was unanimous.

"Have it your way," he said, satisfied that he could achieve his ends whichever way they acted. "Let's leave the hosses here and walk up peaceable and friendly-like. It might not be the right folk. If it is, we'll throw down on 'em by surprise. Only watch that short-growed Creole. He's a regular snake."

Accepting the plan, five of the men dismounted. They handed their reins to the sixth, he who had raised the first protest. Leaving him with two horses on one side and three at the other, they formed into a rough half circle with Widge at its center and slouched toward the table.

Studying the newcomers' appearances and behavior, Dolman felt uneasy. He knew enough about western conventions to be aware of their breach of accepted etiquette. Custom and politeness should have dictated that they request permission before approaching what amounted to another party's campsite.

Glancing quickly at de Froissart, while easing his chair around so that he was facing the quintet with his legs clear of the table, Dolman decided that he was uneasy and decided that he had good cause. The Creole did not have his Remington Double Derringers on his person. If the men should be contemplating mischief, he would be dependent upon his sword-cane. That could not be a comforting thought when he would be opposed by men who were all wearing firearms.

For his part, Dolman kept both hands in plain sight on the table. While none of the men struck him as being a top gun, they had him too heavily outnumbered for him to make hostile gestures.

"Danged if we ain't forgetting our manners, boys," the lanky man said, coming to a stop about ten feet from the table. He touched the brim of his hat with his right hand, looking at de Froissart. "We should've asked you if we could light 'n' rest our saddles, mister. Hope there's no offense took?"

"None taken," the Creole answered, noticing that all the men were watching him, and not displeased by the way they clearly regarded him as the most important member of his party. He looked to where his valet was standing by the open picnic basket on the boot of the coach. "I don't think we've enough food—"

"Shucks," Widge interrupted, making a brief depreciatory gesture. "That warn't why we stopped. Seeing's how we've got us some cattle to sell, we was wondering if you-all's the folks from the Pilar Hide & Tallow Company?"

"We are," de Froissart confirmed.

"I told you they was," Widge declared, turning to the man at his right. "So we might's well get on with it."

On swinging to face the table again, the lanky man showed that he had done more than address his companions. He held his army Colt and, cocking back its hammer, pointed the barrel at the Creole's chest. For a moment he considered firing immediately but decided to wait. His companions would be more inclined to start throwing lead if the Creole tried to resist their demands to be given the payroll that Laxterby—the name Roxterby had been using in the days when he had known Widge—had claimed was in the coach.

Four more hands closed on and raised revolvers from their holsters. While none of the men had drawn fast, Dolman had been lulled into a sense of false security. Taken by surprise, he continued to sit motionless. It was obvious to him, however, that they regarded de Froissart as being the most dangerous person at the table. The man at the right was covering Dolman, and the one on the left had his attention on the Negroes. All the other three were lining their weapons at the Creole.

De Froissart no longer found his preeminence an attractive proposition. Being uncomfortably aware of his only weapon's limitations under the circumstances, he hoped that—with three cocked revolvers directed at him—Dolman would not be foolish enough to offer resistance. If he did, de Froissart would almost certainly be the first one the men would kill.

That same thought was also occurring to the Captain, but he could not see any way in which he might turn it to his advantage.

3

PROFACI WAS TALKING
TO GOMEZ

Although Austin Viridian had walked from his home that morning, he took one of the horses from the factory's corral for the return journey. By doing so, he hoped that he would be able to terminate his business in time to reach the stream before Gianna Profaci had finished her work and left.

The town of Pilar straddled the Houston to Fort Worth stagecoach trail, being about half a mile north of the factory and just beyond the upper end of the gorge. While somewhat more prosperous, due to the revenue brought in by the company, it differed little in general appearance from numerous other small communities that were scattered across the war-impoverished state of Texas.

Closest to the factory, at which the majority of the men found employment, the adobe *jacales,* which had been assigned to the Negroes, lay on the gentle slope between the trail and the river. They formed what amounted to a separate, self-contained village.

Beyond the colored-people's section, lining both sides of the trail, stood the town's business premises. They were few in number—the stageline's depot, a livery barn owned by Profaci, a small rooming house, the New Orleans Saloon, Schweitzer's General Store, and the adobe building that served as town hall, courthouse, constable's office, and jail being prominent among them—but supplied most of the residents' and visitors' needs. The white population had their homes in an untidy cluster to the east of the main, in fact only, street.

Although de Froissart and Schweitzer lived at their business establishments, the Viridians and Profacis occupied more palatial quarters. Each family had a colonial-style mansion that had been built under the Italian's guidance, before the War Between the States. Erected in the woodland behind the town, each property was separated from its neighbor and practically hidden by the trees.

Even before Viridian had reached the outskirts of the town, he saw several men following a small boy from the saloon. One pointed and the rest looked in his direction. Watching them start talking, he guessed that he was the topic of their conversation. Urging his mount to a faster pace, he studied the party and identified them as citizens. One of them was the town constable, and another, Viridian noticed without enthusiasm, was the man de Froissart had hired three weeks earlier to be his saloon's floor boss.

Tall, broad-shouldered, dark-haired, and swarthily handsome, Jesse Sparlow dressed in the fashion of a Mississippi riverboat gambler. He was said to be fast with the ivory-handled army Colt in the high cavalry twist-hand holster on the left side of his waist belt. He had many qualities that annoyed Viridian: education, excellent manners and various other social graces. What was more, he invariably treated the hide and tallow man with a thinly veiled condescension that suggested that only his position as a partner in the company made him worthy of consideration. It was not an attitude calculated to endear him to Viridian.

There was nothing of Sparlow's well-dressed elegance about Joshua Hubric. Big, overweight, clad in worn, untidy town clothes, with an old navy Colt tucked into the waist of his trousers in a way that precluded any hope of it being drawn swiftly, he was neither an efficient nor an effective peace officer. He owed his position to being distantly related to Marlene Viridian, it having been decided that he could do less harm as constable than in any other capacity.

"Howdy, Mr. Viridian," Sparlow said in greeting as the hide and tallow man drew up and dismounted. He indicated the youngster who was standing in the forefront of the crowd. "The boy just came and told us he'd heard some shooting at the factory."

"I was fixing to get me a posse and come to see what was up, Cousin Austin," Hubric went on. "Only—"

"I figured there couldn't have been anything serious happening, when I saw you coming in at a walk," Sparlow interrupted. "Has there been some trouble out there?"

"Some," Viridian admitted, taking no more notice of Hubric than to hand him the horse's reins. "Ribagorza's getting greedy."

With that, the hide and tallow man told an attentive audience what had happened at the factory. He could see that they were startled and perturbed by what they heard. However, it was Sparlow's reaction that attracted most of his interest. At the mention of Gomez's name, the gambler frowned.

"Gomez," Sparlow said, when the explanation had come to its end. "Well, I'll be damned!"

"What's up?" Viridian asked.

"We'd best send some of these fellers out to help guard the factory," Sparlow stated, ignoring the question.

"See to it, Hubric," Viridian commanded.

"I didn't want to say anything in front of them," Sparlow declared, after the constable and the other men had moved away. "But I went over to Bryan last Saturday to take a look at the kind of business the Two Bulls Saloon's doing. The boss has his eye on it, you know."

"He said something about it," Viridian admitted. "But what's that got to—"

"As I was going in," Sparlow interrupted, in the superior

way that had always antagonized the hide and tallow man, "Joe Profaci was talking to Gomez."

"You saw *Joe Profaci* talking to Gomez?" Viridian repeated, scowling suspiciously. "What were they saying?"

"I wouldn't know," Sparlow replied. "As I went in, the owner came across to meet me. Then Gomez looked, said something, and got up and left by the back door."

"Did Profaci tell you what they'd been talking about?"

"No. Before I could get away from the owner, he'd gone out of the side door and I didn't see him again. Not that I thought anything about it at the time. I knew Gomez worked for Ribagorza. And Profaci doesn't come to the New Orleans all that often, so we don't know each other too well."

"Likely not," Viridian grunted.

"Anyway, I'm not saying that there was anything wrong with them being together," Sparlow pointed out, nodding to where Hubric was talking in an excited, yet pleading fashion, with the other men. "It was just that I thought it wouldn't be wise to let them know what I'd seen."

"What's holding you up there?" Viridian demanded, glaring at the constable.

"These fellers can't make up their minds who should be coming with me," Hubric answered petulantly.

"I'll see to it," Sparlow promised, and strode away.

Watching the gambler approach the other men, Viridian scowled and thought of what he had been told. Before he could draw any conclusions, the door of Schweitzer's General Store opened. Followed by the owner, Gianna Profaci walked out. They came to a halt on the sidewalk, staring at the men on the street with considerable interest. Looking at them, Viridian felt a surge of annoyance. Clearly he had arrived too late to meet the Italian woman in the privacy of the woods.

"Is something wrong, Austin?" the storekeeper asked.

The oldest and by far the richest of the partners, Bernard Schweitzer rarely dressed in anything other than a shabby, rumpled and almost threadbare black suit, or donned a collar and tie. In his late fifties, he was plump, going bald and sported steel-rimmed spectacles that conveyed an aura of benevolence that was far removed from his true nature. Over the years he had gained a well-deserved reputation for being a shrewd and frequently ruthless businessman.

"Yes," Viridian admitted, walking toward the couple. His gaze roamed over the woman in a lascivious manner, although he was speaking to his partner, and he grew more angry as he thought of the pleasures that would not be available to him that afternoon. "We've got trouble on our hands, Bernie."

Standing with her right hand resting gracefully on her hip, Gianna Profaci was well worth Viridian's scrutiny. A few years younger than Marlene, Gianna matched her in height and physique. What was more, she did not attempt to conceal her physical attractions. Shoulder-long, glossy black hair framed an olive-skinned face that was beautiful, sultry, and suggestive of her tempestuous nature. The rich, full curves of her gorgeous body were emphasized by a snug-fitting, multicolored blouse and tight black satin skirt from beneath which her bare feet peeped coyly. Unless Viridian missed his guess, she was as usual wearing very little underneath the two garments.

"When do we have anything else these days?" Schweitzer groaned, aware of how his partner was looking at the woman by his side. He raised his eyes to the sky as if in search of strength. "What is it this time?"

"I'll tell you inside," Viridian replied. "You'd better stay as well, Gianna. I thought you'd be doing your washing and was going to send for you."

"No, I didn't go today," the woman replied, flickering a glance at the men on the street. "Everybody looks excited."

"They've reason to be," Viridian stated, wishing to impress his partner with the serious nature of the danger that seemed likely to threaten them. "Shall we go in?"

Crossing the large main room of the building, with its miscellany of goods on display, Gianna and Viridian waited for Schweitzer to unlock and open the door to his private office. He waved for them to enter and waited until they did so, then followed and closed the door. There were thick steel bars at the office's window, and the second door—which was the rear exit —was secured by two bolts and a lock. The furnishings were simple and far from luxurious; a rolltop desk, a table, half a dozen rickety chairs, and a massive safe. The latter, holding the company's operating finances, was the reason for the precautions against unauthorized entry.

"You did right not to pay," Schweitzer declared at the end of Viridian's story of the incident. "But he's not going to like what's happened."

"That's for sure," the burly man agreed, pleased that his partner had drawn such a conclusion.

"What I don't see is why Gomez tried to kill you," the storekeeper went on. "What could Ribagorza hope to gain by it?"

"It would've showed the rest of you that he wasn't fooling," Viridian pointed out, having considered the matter along with the rest of the incident as he was riding into town. However, he did not mention the suspicions that Sparlow had aroused. "Then you'd have thought twice about refusing the next time he sent Gomez."

"Do you think he'll try again?" Schweitzer inquired worriedly.

"Don't you?" Viridian countered.

"I do," the storekeeper admitted, which was what the burly man had hoped to hear.

The more Viridian had thought about the matter, both after it had happened and while returning to town, the greater had grown his conviction that Ribagorza would *not* follow up the attempt to obtain an advance payment for the cattle. While tough and unscrupulous, the Mexican was also sufficiently intelligent to realize that the plan had gone wrong. When Gomez did not rejoin the herd, he would guess the truth and expect the partners to take precautions against any reprisals he might be contemplating. Being a businessman, he would conclude that the risks involved in trying to avenge his *segundo* outweighed any possible gains. So he would go to find another market for his wares.

However, as Viridian had seen a way in which he could capitalize upon the incident and use it as a means of obtaining money from the company, he had hoped that the storekeeper would not duplicate his line of reasoning. Certainly nobody else seemed to have drawn similar conclusions. Leathers, Roxterby, Sparlow, Hubric, and the other citizens had all responded as if they were expecting Ribagorza to launch an attack at any moment. Having seen the townsmen's reactions, Schweitzer was likely to have had his reasoning influenced along the required lines. What was more, having had less dealings with the Mexican, he lacked Viridian's knowledge of Ribagorza's character.

"Mama mia!" Gianna yelped, staring in alarm from one partner to the other. "Joe's away and I'm all alone at home!"

"We'll send some men out to guard you," the storekeeper promised.

"There's only one thing about that, Bernie," Viridian put in, concealing his delight at how things were going so well. Schweitzer had just given him the opening he required. "We don't have enough men to guard our homes, the factory, and the town."

"What do you mean?" Schweitzer asked.

"I've never known Ribagorza to have less than twenty men when he's brought in a herd," Viridian explained. "And for a play like this, he'll most likely have even more than that backing him. In fact Gomez told me he had."

"Do you think he might attack the town, or our homes, Austin?" Gianna inquired.

"He might, if he can't get back at us through the factory," Viridian answered, noticing that her consternation was not going unnoticed by his partner. "He'll want to teach us a lesson and he knows that we own most of the town, so he could come after us that way."

"He might at that," Schweitzer conceded, and his face showed that he appreciated the full implications of what he was hearing. In the event of such an attack, his own premises would be very vulnerable.

"What we need is some extra guns on hand," Viridian hinted.

"Pierre ought to be back by tomorrow," Schweitzer commented, sensing what was coming and that it would cost the company money.

"He's only one man," Viridian reminded the storekeeper, but refrained from mentioning his hope that the Creole would not return alive.

"Maybe Harlow Dolman will be with him," Schweitzer suggested hopefully. "Ribagorza wouldn't dare go against the state police."

"I wouldn't want to count on that," Viridian grunted. "It's not likely Dolman'll have any of his men with him, and the greasers'll start shooting before he can tell them who he is. And if he doesn't come, it will be too late for us to start trying to hire extra guns."

"We won't have time to get them anyway," Schweitzer protested.

"We will, provided we get Roxterby started on it this afternoon," Viridian contradicted. "According to what he told me, he can fetch some in for us and have them here in two days."

"What good will that do?" the storekeeper demanded. "Ribagorza will have arrived and done what he wants to by the time they get here."

"I don't think he'll be here for at least three days," Viridian answered.

"Why?" Schweitzer wanted to know.

"He won't be holding his herd too near, in case things should have gone wrong," Viridian replied. "And he'll stay where he is until Gomez gets back to tell him what's happened. No, I'm betting he's stopped at least two days' drive away and it'll be three at the soonest before he comes."

"You could be right," Schweitzer conceded. "And if you are, he might not come when he realizes what's happened."

"That's not likely." Viridian sniffed. "You know what these greasers are like. Cut one and they all bleed. I'd bet they'll be coming looking for blood as soon as they figure out what's happened to Gomez and his men."

"You've got to get enough men to fight them off, Bernie!"

Gianna insisted, moving forward, with her expressive face showing that she was frightened.

"All right," the storekeeper answered. "Tell Roxterby to go and fetch them, Austin."

"I'll send word for him to come in and get on to it," Viridian promised, and after a brief pause went on, "He's going to need some money."

"How much?" Schweitzer asked warily.

"Five hundred'll do," Viridian replied.

"Five hundred?" Schweitzer yelped.

"Hired guns come a mite higher than nigger factory hands," Viridian pointed out, unmoved by his partner's response. It was pretty well what he had expected, for Schweitzer kept a tight hold on the company's purse strings and hated to part with money under any conditions. "We need ten at least, and they'll not come without cash in their hands. I'd be happier if we could get twenty. That way we'll have the town and the factory safe. Of course, we could leave guarding the town to Josh Hubric and the men. But I aim to have the factory protected."

"But five hundred dollars . . ." Schweitzer began.

"It'll cost a hell of a lot more than that to set right all the damage Ribagorza'll do if we don't have it protected," Viridian pointed out. "And I'm sure as hell not paying out that much from my own pocket. Neither you, Joe, nor Pierre would."

"You give him the money, Bernie Schweitzer!" Gianna ordered. "I know Pierre and Joe would want you to. We need the men to fight them off when they come."

"All right." The storekeeper sighed, yielding in the face of the woman's determination. "I'll give it to you, Austin. But—"

Before the comment could be completed, they heard heavy feet pounding hurriedly across the store. There was a knock at the door, and without waiting to be invited, Leathers and Sparlow entered the office.

"It's Ribagorza, boss," the corral supervisor said, directing his words at Viridian.

"Have you found him already?" Schweitzer almost screeched, remembering that Leathers had been sent to do so.

"I didn't have to," the supervisor replied. "You know Otis Twickery, boss?"

"I know him," Viridian agreed, in tones that implied that the knowledge was anything but a source of pleasure.

"I met him on the trail, bringing some wolves' skins in to sell—" Leathers began.

"Damn it!" Schweitzer snorted. "We could do without that ornery bastard coming at a time like this."

"It's lucky he was coming," Leathers warned. "He reckoned he'd seen Ribagorza headed this way with a fair-sized herd of cattle. Said they ought to be here by sundown tomorrow at the latest."

"Sundown!" Schweitzer repeated, and glared furiously at his partner. "But you said that—."

"Did Twickery tell you anything else?" Viridian demanded, ignoring the comment.

"He allows that Ribagorza's got more men than usual along," Leathers answered. "And from the way they'd set up their camp when he saw them, they were ready to handle trouble should it come."

A furious snarl burst from Viridian as he considered the implications of what he had just heard. Obviously he had been wrong in his estimation of how Ribagorza would react. Clearly the Mexican was meaning to visit the factory and would be very angry when he learned of his *segundo*'s and men's deaths. What was more, to save himself losing face with the remainder of his gang, he could not let the incident pass unpunished.

As Viridian had told his partner, there were insufficient men available to protect the factory, town, and two mansions adequately. What had been merely an excuse to obtain enough money for Roxterby for organizing the murders of Marlene and de Froissart was now a serious factor. Nor was there any way in which they could bring in reinforcements before the Mexicans arrived.

4
WE'VE GOT US A STANDOFF

"Stay put and nobody'll get hurt!" Widge commanded, hoping that de Froissart would not obey and so supply him with an excuse to start shooting.

Instead of obliging, the Creole very sensibly remained motionless.

"We don't aim to hurt none of you-all," promised the man who had warned about the penalty for killing, and he covered Dolman. "We just want the money."

"You're welcome to all I've got," de Froissart declared. "But after a week at the Tarrant County Fair, I've not got much left, and I suppose that applies—"

"That's not what we've been told," protested the outlaw who was keeping an eye on the Negroes. "You're toting your company's payroll—"

"*Payroll?*" the Creole interrupted, throwing a puzzled look at his companions. "I don't understand—"

"Don't try that with us, we *know* you've got it!" Widge spat menacingly and, trying to provoke de Froissart into some action that would justify his death, nodded at Marlene Viridian. "Maybe you want us to ask her where it be?"

"Drop those guns!" ordered a deep, young-sounding, and well-educated Texas drawl that originated from beyond the table and on the woodland's side of the trail.

Hearing the words, the five men confronting Marlene, de Froissart, and Harlow Dolman did not obey immediately. Instead they and the sixth member of their gang—who had remained with the horses—looked at the speaker. They wanted to discover who had intervened and to estimate the full extent of the danger they were facing.

Despite being partially concealed by the massive trunk of a large old oak tree, the man who had spoken was not difficult to locate. In fact he would have been hard to miss under any circumstances. A good six foot three inches in height, even without taking into account his high-heeled, fancy-stitched boots or the low-crowned, wide-brimmed white Texas-style hat —the band of which was decorated by silver conchas—that sat at a jaunty jack-deuce angle on his golden blond, curly hair, he was a youngster who had not yet reached his twentieth birthday. For all that, his tanned, handsome face expressed grim determination to enforce his will.

The newcomer's tan-colored shirt, the scarlet silk bandanna that was tight-rolled and knotted about his throat, and the brown trousers—with their cuffs turned up and hanging outside his boots—might look expensive, but they were the functional working attire of a cowhand. They had obviously been tailored to fit the tremendous spread of his shoulders, slender waist, and long, powerful legs. About his middle hung a well-designed, excellently made brown *buscadero* gunbelt, with an ivory-handled army Colt in each of its contoured, tied-down holsters. It was the kind of rig that a real fast man with a gun would wear.

All in all, the young blonde conveyed an impression of exceptional physical strength without being slow-moving, clumsy, or awkward. He also looked as if he knew exactly what he was doing. Despite the quality of his gunbelt, he was not relying upon the twin Colts to back up his command. Instead, he cra-

dled the butt of a rifle to his right shoulder and gazed along its
barrel.

It was not, the outlaws observed with growing consternation
and alarm, just a single-shot weapon. The tube underneath and
extending the length of the barrel suggested that it was a Henry
repeater. Possibly, if its wooden foregrip was anything to go by,
it was one of the "New Improved" variety—soon to be given
the name by which it would become famous, the "Winchester
Model of 1866"—that had already been featured in the pages of
various dreambooks.*

No matter which type of Henry it might be, such a rifle was
capable of pouring out at least fifteen bullets as fast as the man
using it could operate the loading lever and squeeze the trigger.
For all his youth and somewhat dandified clothes, the blond
giant looked like he could handle it with sufficient speed and
accuracy to be very dangerous.

On hearing Mark Counter's voice coming from behind him,
Dolman stiffened slightly. He glanced swiftly to the left, esti-
mating the distance that was separating him from the coach, and
decided that he could dive underneath it if necessary—and
if he was given the opportunity to do so by the men who were
confronting him.

Having settled what he intended to do if the big blonde's
intervention caused the outlaws to start shooting, the Captain
turned his attention to the other people at the table. From their
tense attitudes and expressions, Marlene and de Froissart were
sharing his anxiety. The woman sat as if she had been turned to
stone, staring at the outlaws. Just as motionless, the Creole also
watched for the first hint of hostile action.

However, the hail of bullets the trio were expecting did not
come. Instead the man who was covering Dolman swung his
gaze at the lanky outlaw. As he did so, he inadvertently allowed the barrel to turn away from the Captain and to sink
until it was pointing to the ground.

"Damn it all, Widge!" Dirk said, in an aggrieved manner.

* *Dreambook:* "a mail-order catalog."

"You reckoned's how there'd only be the Creole with the wom—"

"Shut it!" Widge snarled back.

"You heard me!" Mark called, before the lanky outlaw could say no more. His voice took on a harder note. "Let those guns fall. *Pronto!*"

"Ain't no reason why we should," Widge answered hurriedly, darting glances to his left and right and finding that—as he had expected—his companions were exhibiting signs of alarm. He spoke to prevent them obeying the blond youngster's order. "We've got 'em lined on these good folks here."

That was a point that the big blonde had already taken into consideration while moving silently and unnoticed to take up his position behind the oak tree.

Mark's original intention had never been to try to shoot the turkey but to give Marlene, de Froissart, and Dolman an opportunity to converse in his absence. Suspecting that the Captain was deeply involved in some of the Pilar Hide & Tallow Company's less legal activities, the big blonde had hoped to gather information that would not be mentioned in his presence. Having made a wide half circle through the woodland, he had been moving closer when the outlaws arrived. Like his companions, he had become suspicious. On discovering that his suspicions had been justified, he had prepared to take a hand in the affair.

Following some sound advice that had been given him by Dusty Fog, Mark had thought before acting. He had realized the danger to Marlene, de Froissart, and Dolman if he handled the situation incorrectly. However, studying the opposition, he had formed an assessment of its potential. From the men's appearances and behavior he had deduced that they were petty and not too experienced criminals. While they could be dangerous if given the opportunity, he doubted whether they would be overintelligent or courageous. If he had believed otherwise, he would have remained silent unless it became obvious that they planned to do more than just rob their victims. As it was, he had taken every precaution that he could think of to reduce the risk of harm coming to the people at the table.

"Trouble being, I'm lined on you, full-loaded and all set to go," Mark pointed out. "And, way I see it, it all stands on how many of you're game to get killed. Because, as sure's hell's for sinners, that's just what it'll come to happen, powder starts burning. And I'm standing too far off for them handguns of yours."

Once again Widge flickered looks to find out what his men thought of the situation. He sensed that, even without the blond giant having explained matters, they fully appreciated their peril. Covered by a *repeating* rifle held by a man who was standing a good thirty yards away, which—although his weapon could reach them easily—put him at a distance where they could not count upon hitting him with their revolvers, they realized that resistance would be fraught with danger. If they should throw lead at the men and woman at the table, he would reply in the same fashion. And he held the means to kill every one of them before they could retreat to their horses.

Being aware of the kind of men he had recruited, Widge accepted that there was no longer any hope of robbing the coach and killing its occupants. None of the gang would be inclined to take the sort of chances that were unavoidable to turn the tables on the big youngster.

Nor, if it came to a point, did Widge particularly want to. Having called attention to himself by doing the majority of the talking, he would probably find that he was the young cowhand's first target should lead start flying. He had already received a hundred dollars from "Laxterby." So, even if the gang withdrew peaceably, he would still have something to show for his trouble.

The problem facing Widge was how he might bring about a peaceable withdrawal.

Unaware of the thoughts that were running through his leader's head, the man with the horses—who went by the unflattering name of Dog-Ear—decided that he would help his companions. Releasing the reins he had been given, he reached slowly toward the rifle in his saddleboot. It was only a single-shot Enfield muzzle-loader, but it was still capable of nullifying the advantage of the cowhand's weapon in the matter of range.

Seeing what Dog-Ear was doing, Dolman and de Froissart were both aware of the implications. Watching the rest of the gang, Mark Counter would not become aware of the danger until it was too late. Most likely he would be killed without knowing what had hit him. Neither man would have objected to the big blonde's death under different circumstances, but both could see the danger to themselves. The gang might start to throw lead as soon as their companion's rifle had taken Mark out of the game. However, each of them could visualize what would happen if he tried to warn the young Texan.

"Take your hand off that rifle, *hombre*!" Mark snapped. Appreciating the danger posed by Dog-Ear, he kept glancing at him without taking the Winchester* out of alignment on the main body of the gang. "If it comes out, some of your *amigos*'ll get killed."

Startled by the discovery that he was under observation, Dog-Ear removed his hand from the Enfield's butt and allowed it to slip back into the boot. Sitting upright once more, he made sure that he kept his palms displayed prominently.

Regarding the incident as convincing evidence of the cowhand's competence and control of the situation, Widge conceded that his gang's position was hopeless. He had not suspected that the big blonde was also watching Dog-Ear and had mixed emotions on what had happened. While the horseholder might have broken the deadlock, he could also have caused Widge to be killed.

However, suspecting that life in the state's penitentiary was anything but enjoyable, Widge was not greatly enamored of the prospect of surrender, even though the alternative appeared to be getting shot. With that in mind, he decided to offer a compromise that the youngster might be willing to accept so as to avoid endangering his friends around the table.

* To avoid confusion, the author is using the rifle's better-known name.

"You-all can't gun us down without getting these here good folks shot full of holes, big feller," Widge declared, watching how the words were being received by the men and woman who were to have been his victims, as well as how the cowhand was taking them. "But, again' that, me 'n' the boys ain't exactly looking to get killed neither."

"So?" Mark inquired, sounding far more disinterested than he was feeling.

"It looks like we've got us a standoff," Widge suggested.

Being fully cognizant of the danger that still existed for Marlene, de Froissart, and Dolman, Mark was willing to come to terms if possible. Knowing that for himself to have made an offer might have been interpreted by the outlaws as a sign of weakness, he had held back in the hope that their leader might come up with a solution to the problem.

"You-all sound like a man who's got something on his mind," Mark prompted, still retaining his matter-of-fact tone.

"No harm's been done to nobody," Widge went on. "So, happen the best thing all round'd be for us to go our way and leave you good folks to do likewise."

Despite his earlier fears, Dolman could see that the danger was passing. From what was being said, the outlaws were willing to leave peacefully. He viewed that possibility with mixed feelings, but a desire to do his duty as a peace officer had nothing to do with them. Shooting it out with the gang would have put his life in danger. Against that, they had already considered de Froissart was the most dangerous person at the table. So the outlaws would have made the Creole and Mark Counter their primary targets. If de Froissart had been killed, there would be one less partner between Dolman and control of the Pilar Hide & Tallow Company.

When the Captain first learned of the agreement on the ownership of the company, he realized what it meant to his ambitions. He would have to dispose of the four male partners, leaving Marlene as the sole surviving owner. With that in mind, providing his own life would not have been endangered, he would not have been averse to the gang starting to shoot. De

Froissart would almost certainly have been killed. However, if Mark Counter accepted the outlaw's offer, that would not happen.

Even as Dolman reached his conclusions, he noticed that he was no longer being watched by any of the outlaws. In fact, although the trio were still covering de Froissart, none of them was taking any notice of Dolman. They were dividing their attention between the Creole and Mark Counter, who was standing on the right side of the trail and some distance beyond the table.

Moving his right hand very slowly, Dolman lowered it toward the rosewood butt of the navy Colt in his "clamshell" holster. Hardly daring to breathe, in case doing so might draw unwanted attention his way, he completed the movement without being seen or challenged.

Studying the nervous tension being displayed by the five outlaws who were nearest to the table, the Captain could imagine how the remainder would react if he fired at one of them. Like rats in a trap, they would start to fight back. If good luck favored Dolman, Mark Counter would be killed as a bonus to de Froissart.

Dolman realized that to start shooting would involve a certain risk to himself. However, he considered that he had one thing in his favor. Having opened fire, he would be ready to avoid the consequences. Unfortunately he could see that the same would not apply to Marlene. There was no way in which he could warn her of his intentions. She would, he concluded sourly as he thought of how she had treated him since meeting Mark Counter, have to take her chance. If the worst happened, he could always use Gianna Profaci—with whom he was also on excellent terms—as the means to attaining his end. If anything, the Italian woman would be easier to handle.

Having decided what to do, Dolman waited to hear how the blond giant would respond to the lanky outlaw's offer. Once he knew that, he could make his move accordingly.

"I'll go along with you on that," Mark declared, knowing a refusal might cause the gang to panic and start throwing lead.

"How's it stand with you, mister?" Widge asked, remembering what he had been told about the Creole's ability as a fighting man and looking at him.

"I've no intention of trying to stop you leaving," de Froissart stated, relaxing.

Although the Creole's voice showed his relief, Dolman had found a new source of anxiety. If the gang's leader looked at him, the position of his right hand would be a warning of his intentions. He wondered if he should remove it and forget what he had hoped to do. Before the Captain reached a decision, Mark spoke and prevented any of the outlaws from looking at him.

"Back off real slow and easy," the big blonde ordered, wanting to see the men on their way before anything could go wrong. "And keep the barrels of your guns pointed at the ground."

"Do like the gent says, boys," Widge advised, accepting that Mark was taking a reasonable precaution. While offering the people at the table a measure of protection against treachery, it would not leave the gang defenseless. "They'll play square."

Listening to the arrangements, Dolman wondered if he should allow the men to start carrying out Mark's instructions before making his move. To do so might reduce the danger to himself, but it would also improve de Froissart's chances of survival. Not only that, none of the outlaws were looking at him. Their attention was directed mainly upon the big blonde. There would be more chance of somebody noticing what he was doing as they were backing away.

Having drawn his conclusions, Dolman stabbed his forefinger through the Colt's trigger guard and on to the holster's switch. Instantly the mechanism operated and set the revolver free. Tilting the seven-and-a-half-inch-long barrel upward, he cocked the action with his thumb.

Hearing the familiar triple clicking sound, Dirk became aware that all was far from being well. Yet he could not believe that he was in danger. In addition to having decided that Dolman was a harmless dude, he had felt sure the other could not draw a revolver without having to rise or otherwise making his intentions obvious.

What the outlaw did not know, never having seen one, was the advantage a "clamshell" had over practically every other type of butt-to-the-rear holster. The weapon could be extracted from it just as easily and swiftly when its user was seated as would be possible when he was standing.

To add to Dirk's alarm and consternation, he found that his revolver was no longer pointing at the "dude." Before he could rectify the situation, there was a sharp crack, and smoke belched from the muzzle of Dolman's Colt. The Captain had taken the extra split second to make sure of his aim, and his bullet struck the outlaw between the eyes. Dirk was jolted backward and killed instantly. Although his forefinger tightened spasmodically on the trigger, the bullet flew harmlessly into the air as he fell.

Having removed the most immediate threat to himself, Dolman dived sideways and down. Even as he started to disappear under the coach, he heard startled exclamations. These were echoed almost immediately by the crash of detonating black powder, but none of the bullets came his way. He hoped that the sounds meant de Froissart was a victim and wondered briefly how Marlene was faring. Not that he tried to look and find out. He was too busy, wriggling rapidly beneath the vehicle.

Realizing what Dolman's action would cause to happen, de Froissart grabbed for his sword-cane and tried to rise. By doing so, he ensured that the outlaws' attention would be drawn his way. Although they had been on the point of withdrawing, Widge and the man on either side of him responded as the Captain had predicted. Spitting out curses, they fired their weapons practically in unison. By pure chance, rather than accurate aim, none of the heavy-caliber bullets missed their mark. Hurled backward with three holes in his chest, de Froissart was dead before his body struck the ground.

For her part, Marlene had already decided what she would try to do if there was any trouble. However, like de Froissart, she had believed that Mark had ended the matter without it. Although she had caught Dolman's surreptitious movements from the corner of her eye, the idea that he might be contemplating drawing and shooting had not occurred to her. She had thought that he was merely taking a precaution, perhaps an ill-advised one, against treachery by the outlaws.

Then she had seen the Colt lifting into alignment!

Momentarily Marlene had still not believed that Dolman would fire. To do so would ruin all hope of the outlaws departing peacefully and put her party's lives in deadly peril.

While the shot caught Marlene unprepared, she recovered quickly and showed remarkable presence of mind. Even as de Froissart was killed, she jumped to her feet. Sending her chair flying and overturning the table, she spun around and flung herself toward the rear end of the coach. Instantly the man who had been keeping the Negroes under observation started to swing the barrel of his revolver in her direction.

Once safely underneath the coach, Dolman crawled rapidly to the other side. The thunder of guns continued, but still nobody was firing at him. Emerging, he rose and looked at his Colt, not that he intended to take any further part in the fighting at that moment. He meant to let Mark Counter bear the brunt of the outlaws' attack and to finish off the survivors after they had disposed of the big youngster. With that thought in mind, he returned the revolver and closed the flap of the holster. Then he looked to where his Henry rifle was in the boot of his McClellan saddle. That would be a more suitable weapon for what he had in mind.

Up until the moment that Dolman fired, Mark was confident that he had brought about a satisfactory settlement. Taken by surprise, he was unable to save de Froissart. Noticing the man who was attempting to draw a bead on Marlene, he changed his point of aim from Widge. He sighted and fired just as the man was starting to squeeze the trigger. Entering the outlaw's throat, the flat-nosed .44 bullet broke his neck. It spun him around and caused his own lead to fly by the woman. Then she passed around the end of the coach, and Mark knew that she would be safe for the time being. His own position was far less secure and was growing more dangerous by the second.

"Rush the big bastard!" Widge screeched, knowing that there was no chance of them reaching the horses while covered by the blond youngster's repeating rifle. "He can't down us all."

Accepting their leader's advice, the remaining pair of dismounted outlaws started to run forward. They fired as they advanced, and although running was not conducive to accuracy, lead screamed by Mark's head. Satisfied that Marlene was temporarily out of danger, he turned his attention to protecting himself.

Without the need for conscious guidance, Mark's right hand had already pivoted the Winchester's lever through its reloading cycle. Showing no sign of being frightened, or even flustered by the near misses, he lined his sights on Widge. He was counting on Dolman, who had started the affair, to help out with the other members of the gang.

What the big blonde did not realize was that Dolman had no intention of shooting until after he had been killed by the outlaws.

5

YOU MIGHT HAVE GOT ME KILLED!

Although Widge's companions had dashed forward on his orders, he did not go with them. Conscious of the blond giant's rifle swinging in his direction, he allowed them to advance and weaved behind the man at his right. Remembering what had happened to Dirk, he guessed that the "dude" might prove more dangerous than they had expected. In which case, the attack was doomed to failure. With that in mind, he turned toward the waiting horses. They were showing their alarm at the disturbance by snorting and swinging away, but Dog-Ear had managed to grab hold of the reins of Widge's mount so as to prevent it from bolting.

With his rifle's sights seeking out Widge, Mark Counter saw him disappear behind the outlaw nearest to the coach's side of the trail. Expecting Dolman to appear and continue what he had so recklessly—as Mark thought—started, the youngster gave his attention to the other member of the gang. Running faster than his companion, he was rapidly approaching a distance at which he might be expected to make a hit with his revolver. Keeping the barrel moving until it was aiming in the required direction, Mark tightened his right forefinger and drove a bullet into the man's head. There was a spray of splintered bone, blood, and shattered brains, and the stricken outlaw collapsed as if he had been boned.

Flame and smoke gushed from the second outlaw's weapon. Feeling the wind of the bullet fan his cheek as he was working the Winchester's lever, Mark could not help stepping sideways. He was compelled to lower the rifle from his shoulder to keep it from striking against the trunk of the tree. Thinking fast, he decided that to return to his original position would be both foolish and dangerous.

Still assuming that Dolman would take a hand, Mark swung to his right and darted swiftly around the tree. He burst into view of the trail in time to see Widge racing toward the horses. There was still no sign of Dolman, however.

Then the big blonde came close to being killed!

Unaware of his leader's desertion, the remaining outlaw had anticipated what Mark was doing and cut loose with a shot on his reappearance. Caught high in the crown by the bullet, the youngster's hat was thrust from his head. Snapping against his throat, its *barbiquejo* chin strap prevented it from leaving him entirely, and it dangled on his back. Snarling curses, the man began to thumb back the hammer of his revolver to try again.

When Marlene had seen Widge turning instead of accompanying his companions, she did not hesitate. Darting around the coach so as to put its body between her and the lanky outlaw, she found herself confronted by Harlow Dolman.

"Do something!" the woman screeched, staring at his empty right hand. "One of—"

"I'll get my Henry," the Captain replied, without letting her finish the warning.

Before Marlene could say any more, Dolman went by her and looked cautiously toward the trail. What he saw caused him to emerge from behind the coach and start moving toward where the weapon lay in its boot on his saddle.

There was no time for Mark to return the butt of the rifle to his shoulder. With it held no higher than waist level and pointed by instinctive alignment, he started to fire as swiftly as he could operate the mechanism. Unlike the Spencer, its only serious rival in the repeater field, the Winchester did not require its hammer to be cocked manually. So it could produce a very rapid rate of fire in skilled hands, one that was highly disconcerting and unnerving to a man who was confronted by it.

Six times in four seconds a cartridge was detonated and lead was blasted from the Winchester's muzzle. Turning the barrel slightly while blurring the lever up and down, but before each pressure on the trigger, Mark sent the bullets in an arc that encompassed his assailant. Caught by the third, fourth, and fifth of them, with his own weapon cocked but unfired, the outlaw went spinning like a child's top away from the big blonde. He flung aside the revolver involuntarily. It went off harmlessly in the air and, oozing blood from a trio of holes in his torso, he crashed lifeless on to the grass at the side of the trail.

Automatically manipulating the rifle's lever and replenishing its chamber, Mark saw Dolman appear with empty hands from behind the coach. Guessing that the Captain was going to collect the Henry, the youngster turned his attention to Widge. Instead of trying to avenge his companions' deaths, the lanky man was deserting them.

With the rest of the horses scattering like quail that had been startled into flight, Dog-Ear set his own and Widge's mounts into motion. Seeing the sole survivor of his gang approaching, the lanky man dropped his Colt. He heard the revolver shots that preceded and followed the rapid blast of the Winchester's response but did not look back. Instead he converged with his horse, caught its saddlehorn in both hands, and swung himself around, then astride its back. Once there, seeing that he had only Dog-Ear left, he snatched his reins from the other's hands and turned his mount to the right. Giving a yell and applying further encouragement with his spurs, he sent the animal bounding into the woodland. Followed by Dog-Ear, he headed at an ever-increasing pace up the slope and selected a route that he hoped would put trees or bushes between himself and the big blonde's rifle.

Whipping the Winchester to his shoulder, Mark did not fire. Already Widge was leaving the trail and was among the trees before he could take aim. Nor did he attempt to shoot at Dog-Ear. An efficient gunfighter, Mark did not kill for the sake of killing. If the pair had tried to attack him, he would have gunned them down without hesitation. Seeing that they were fleeing, he was content to let them go; especially as there was a chance that one of the others might still be able to continue the fight. Wounded and without any means of escape, such a man would be as dangerous as a boxed-in and stick-teased diamond-back rattlesnake.

With that sobering thought in mind, Mark looked along his rifle's barrel from one to another of the quartet. From all appearances, the only person to whom they were going to cause trouble was the undertaker, who would have to come and collect their bodies for burial. That figured. Under the circumstances there had been no hope for more merciful shooting. It had been a case of going for an instantaneous kill to save Marlene's or his own life. Obviously Dolman had been equally unable, or was disinclined, to try to capture his victim injured, but alive.

Satisfied that the danger had passed, for the fleeing pair showed no suggestion that they might be considering halting and resuming the fight, Mark looked at the other members of his party. The Negro driver was hanging on to the lead ropes of his team and preventing them from bolting. Although they were snorting and moving restlessly, Mark's bloodbay stallion and Dolman's bay gelding were so accustomed to the restrictions placed upon their movements by being hobbled that they made no attempt to run away. De Froissart was lying supine and motionless. Studying the blood that spread across the front of his white shirt, Mark assumed that he was dead. The Creole's valet hurried forward and knelt alongside him.

However, Marlene and Dolman attracted most of Mark's interest. Although the Captain had reached the McClellan sad-

dle, he left the Henry in its boot. Instead he turned to face
Marlene as she stalked from behind the coach. Being unaware
that Dolman had fired without justification, Mark was worried
by the woman's furious expression. He wondered if she was
holding him responsible for her narrow escape and would terminate their friendship. Only by retaining it could he hope to
complete his assignment, so he hoped that she would not. One
thing he knew for sure, Dolman would use the incident in an
attempt to discredit him and to lose him Marlene's good offices.

"Why the hell did you have to shoot that man?" the woman
hissed, and to his delight, Mark saw that her furious words
were directed at Dolman. "You might have got *me* killed!"

"Hey, Dolman!" the big blonde barked, taking his cue from
Marlene and cutting in before the Captain could defend himself
against her comment. "What the hell did you have to gun that
feller down for? I had them all set to back out peaceful until
you pulled that fool play."

"I—!" Dolman spluttered, looking from Marlene to Mark
and back as they converged upon him.

."It's no damned thanks to *you* that Marlene wasn't killed
along with Pierre there," Mark continued, ranging himself in a
protective fashion alongside the woman. He was determined to
press home his advantage, so went on, "After you'd started the
fuss, you just dived into your hidey-hole and left her to face
him. One of 'em was all set to down her when I dropped him."

Anger wiped all the handsome lines from Dolman's face as
he watched the way Marlene was reacting to the blond giant's
words. Knowing her, the Captain realized that rather than aris-
ing out of anger or concern over de Froissart's death, her wrath
had been caused by the fright she had received. She was far too
self-centered to care about what happened to the Creole, particularly once she remembered that his demise meant there was
one less partner to share in the profits of the company.

When preparing to kill the outlaw, Dolman had been counting upon Marlene—if she survived—to take the latter factor
into consideration. She would have done so if she had been
allowed time to cool down, particularly if the blond youngster

had died. Unfortunately he had survived and was reminding her of how Dolman had left her to face the danger after having created it. So the necessary cooling-off period had not happened.

"If you'd started shooting instead of talking to them—" Dolman began, in the hope that he could lay the blame on his rival.

"They'd have killed you all where you sat," Mark finished for him.

"You had them covered!" Dolman snarled.

"And they were lining guns on you three, up so close that they'd not be likely to miss," Mark pointed out, deftly countering the unfinished allegation. "That's why I handled it the way I did. Had it been just you and Pierre at the table, I could've played things your way. But, with *Marlene* sitting there, I figured it'd be best to try and get them to pull out peaceable. That way no harm'd come to her. Damn it, they'd've gone, too, if you hadn't spooked and thrown lead at them."

"I'm a captain in the state police!" Dolman answered, desperately seeking an excuse that might exculpate him in Marlene's eyes. "Was I supposed to just sit there and let them rob me?"

"They'd forgotten about doing that when you cut loose," Mark replied. "And because you did, Pierre's dead. On top of which, you put Marlene's life in danger and didn't do one li'l damned thing except get hid when the lead started flying."

An even greater fury boiled inside Dolman as a surreptitious glance at the woman informed him of how thoroughly he was having the ground cut from under his feet.

"Are you blaming me for Pierre's death?" the Captain demanded, avoiding any reference to having endangered Marlene.

"You sure's hell didn't do anything that kept him alive," Mark answered. "And you did even less to stop them trying to kill Marlene. It looked to me like you was counting on that happening to keep the owlhoots busy while you got hid away."

More rage distorted Dolman's face, and his right hand started moving closer to the Colt in its "clamshell" holster. Nobody, he told himself, would blame him if he took violent

exception to such insulting words. Once he had avenged himself upon the big blonde, he felt sure that he could soon bring
Marlene to a more amenable frame of mind.

Suddenly Dolman became aware that the blond youngster
was anything but unprepared to deal with the kind of response
he was contemplating. Although the Winchester was resting
across the crook of his bent left arm, his right hand—its thumb
and fingers slightly bent ready to close—was hovering over the
ivory butt of his off-side Colt. Everything about his stance and
attitude suggested that he was poised, ready to draw and start
shooting. Obviously he was aware of the chance that had been
presented to him and was willing to use it as an excuse to
remove a rival for Marlene's affections.

Remembering the result of the shooting contest they had
held the previous night, Dolman realized that Mark was confident of success. For all his earlier pretense that the result had
been meaningless, the Captain was revising his opinion. He
knew the big Texan was faster and more accurate. What was
more, he had been given proof that the other was capable of
killing. Three of the gang had fallen to his rifle.

Even before shooting the outlaw, Dolman had killed two
men in what he had claimed to be the line of duty. So he was
aware of his own potential in that field. However, he was
equally conscious of the fact that none of his victims had been
expecting him to throw down on them. That did *not* apply to
the blond youngster.

One question that Dolman asked himself was whether Mark
would dare to shoot down a captain of the state police, even in
what could later be passed off as self-defense?

Studying the cowhand, Dolman believed that he might take
the chance. Although he was standing apparently relaxed, he
was as ready to burst into motion as a compressed coil spring.
None of the Captain's earlier victims—and they had been no
more than that—had looked so menacing or dangerous. Nor
had they expected to have to defend themselves. What was
more, in her present frame of mind—which Counter would
ensure endured—Marlene would back up any story he chose to

tell. Nobody would doubt their veracity, even if they claimed that it had been one of the outlaws who had killed Dolman.

For several seconds Dolman continued to stand with his right hand a scant three inches from the butt of his Colt. He met Mark's gaze and attempted to stare him down. If he could divert the big blonde's attention for a split second, he could draw. However, there was an aura of self-confidence about the cowhand that was unnerving. It was the attitude of a man who felt sure that he was the master of the situation.

Finding that he could no longer meet the big Texan's disconcerting scrutiny, Dolman looked away. Inadvertently his eyes strayed to the outlaws' bodies. The sight did nothing to increase his courage. He remembered all too vividly that the man confronting him had put three of them down; two while they were rushing toward him with blazing guns and intent on killing him.

Such a man would not hesitate to take a rival's life!

Dolman suspected that the blond giant was ready, willing, more than able, and very eager to do just that.

While the Captain no longer had the courage to carry out his intentions regarding the youngster, he was equally averse to letting Marlene see him back down. If she did, he would lose any hope of regaining his position with her. Yet there did not seem to be any way in which he could avoid one or the other alternative.

Unless—

Sensing that there might be trouble, Marlene had withdrawn a few steps from the blonde's side so as to be out of the line of fire. If she could be persuaded to intervene, the affair might yet be brought to a bloodless conclusion and without an excessive loss of face for Dolman. That might happen, provided he reminded her in the proper way about his most recent service for the Pilar Hide & Tallow Company.

"I started shooting because the man with the horses matched the description of Paul Dover's killer, Marlene," Dolman stated, allowing his right hand to move slowly away from the

Colt's butt. He saw the woman stiffen and her lips tighten as he spoke and continued. "I'd sign a statement to that effect."

"Do tell," Mark drawled mockingly, having noticed the response from Marlene.

"He'd already murdered Dover and one of his own men, who couldn't have escaped," Dolman went on, watching Marlene and ignoring the comment. "How could we trust a man like that to keep his word?"

Until the Captain had addressed her, Marlene had not been displeased by the turn of events and was willing to let the men settle their differences. Having watched the contest between them, she had no doubts about the outcome. She had already concluded that Dolman was not the partner she required, but was equally aware of his ambitions regarding the company. The incident at the table had been convincing evidence of how far he would go to achieve them. He had been willing to risk sacrificing her to bring about de Froissart's death. Remembering how he had deliberately endangered her life, she would not have been averse to seeing him killed—particularly as his death would have strengthened her hold over Mark.

Listening to Dolman's reference to the possible identity of the outlaw, Marlene knew exactly what was implied. It had been to remind her of the documents they had been discussing just before the arrival of the gang. Perhaps Dolman had placed his copy in the hands of somebody he trusted and had left instructions for its disposal if anything should happen to him. She did not dare take the chance that he had failed to make such a precaution. In which case she had to prevent Mark from killing him.

"If you was trying to down that jasper," Mark said offensively, "you're sure a lousy shot. And he didn't look like—"

"Arguing among ourselves won't bring Pierre back!" Marlene put in hurriedly, adopting what she hoped would be a conciliatory tone. Although she took a step forward, she did not move between the two men in case her peace making should fail. Looking at Mark in a pleading manner, she went on. "I'm sure Harlow thought he was acting for the best."

"I did," Dolman agreed, trying without success to prevent the relief he was feeling from entering his voice. "I thought the one with the horses was Paul Dover's killer."

While the big blonde did not show it, he, too, was pleased that Marlene had interceded. Despite wishing to keep in her good books, he had good reasons for not wanting to force Dolman into a gunfight. The state police would be disinclined to allow a Texan—especially one with Mark's connections—to get away with gunning down one of their number, even in self-defense. Once they started an investigation, Mark's true status would be revealed. In which case, even if he escaped their vengeance, there would be no hope of him proving Viridian's guilt. Another, equally important factor was that Ole Devil Hardin's political enemies would not be slow to try to use the killing as a means of discrediting him.

With those thoughts in mind, Mark had gambled that—recollecting the result of their contest—Dolman would avoid a confrontation. While that had happened, the Captain had contrived to make Marlene intervene. Her intercession had surprised Mark, who would not have suspected her of possessing a forgiving nature. In fact he had expected her to want Dolman punished for placing her in such deadly peril.

Considering the words that had brought about Marlene's change of heart, that she should have taken such an attitude struck Mark as significant. Up to Dolman's reference to the outlaw's identity, she had been clearly willing to let the affair run its course. Thinking back to Dusty Fog's comments on the obvious lies that Dolman had told as an excuse for failing to capture Dover's murderer, Mark decided that their theory of collusion had been correct. He also decided to test how strongly Marlene desired to keep the Captain from harm.

"That being the case," the big blonde challenged, "why'd you drop the other *hombre* and give him the chance to get away?"

"The man I shot was covering Marlene—" Dolman began, gritting out the words.

"Anyways," Mark interrupted, having no intention of letting

such an excuse be elaborated upon, "there's some's'd say, you being a peace officer and all, you should be heading after that feller, seeing's you already lost him after he'd killed Paul Dover."

"My horse isn't saddled," Dolman replied, clenching his fists until their knuckles showed white. "By the time I've done it, they'll be so far away that I won't have a hope of catching them."

"So you're going to lose the feller who you started the whole fuss over and near on got Marlene killed over," Mark scoffed. "Lordy lord! I've always heard the state police—"

"It wasn't Harlow's fault that the man escaped," Marlene put in hurriedly, seeing that Dolman was almost quivering with rage and afraid that he might not be able to control his temper. "The rest of them could have killed you if he hadn't helped—"

"He didn't do so all-fired much to help me," Mark pointed out. "All he did was—"

"Please, Mark!" Marlene gasped, changing her tactics. "I—I don't feel so good. I—I want to get away from here."

"Of course you do, Marlene," Dolman commiserated, hoping that by doing so he would regain some of the ground he had lost. He also realized that there was less danger of being provoked into drawing while they were traveling. "We'll go straight away."

"Looks like you're forgetting something, *mister*," Mark drawled insolently.

"What's that?" Dolman snapped, fighting to control the rage that was boiling inside him and threatened to erupt despite his knowledge that for it to do so would get him killed.

"Those fellers I had to kill because you was so all-fired eager to do your duty as a peace officer," Mark answered, indicating the bodies with a jerk of his right thumb that did not take the hand too far from the butt of its Colt, "it wouldn't be right to just leave them lying there."

"I'll send a wagon to collect them when we get to the next way station." Dolman growled, scowling malevolently but avoiding meeting Mark's challenging gaze.

"The one we was at last night's a whole heap closer," Mark pointed out, successfully maintaining his truculent attitude and conveying the impression that he would like nothing better than to make Dolman draw. "I reckon you'd best go back there and do it."

Once again Marlene could see the possibility of trouble flaring up. Knowing how arrogant and bad-tempered Dolman could be, she was afraid that the blond youngster might goad him to the point where he would act without thinking of the consequences.

"Mark has a good point, Harlow," the woman stated, drawing an angry frown from the Captain. "You could send for the bodies and make a start at hunting the men who escaped much sooner from there."

"If you want my advice," Mark went on, his voice implying that it had better be taken, "you'll go there. Or are you saying it's not the closest place?"

"Did you get the turkey for me, Mark?" Marlene asked, saying the first thing to come into her head in the hope of preventing Dolman from being forced to answer.

"Nope," the big blonde admitted. "I was sneaking up on him when those jaspers arrived. But I didn't like the look of them, so I let him be and came back. How about it, *mister*. Is the place—"

"Would you go and ask the driver to hitch up the team, Mark?" Marlene interrupted, indicating the bodies and giving a convincing shudder. "I want to leave this place. It's horrible being here after—"

"Sure I will, hon—Marlene," Mark declared, but did not turn. Instead he looked at Dolman in a challenging fashion. "You still haven't answered—"

Marlene's nerves were stretched so taut that it was all she could do to prevent herself from screaming. She feared that Mark might achieve his purpose and force a confrontation with Dolman unless she separated them. If the Captain was compelled to reply and chose to disagree, Mark would pretend to take it that he was being called a liar. In Texas at that time, such a charge almost invariably resulted in gunplay.

"Please, Mark!" Marlene almost shrieked, and the strain she was enduring caused a pleading tone to enter her voice. "I want to leave as quickly as possible."

"Anything to oblige *you,* honey," the big blonde drawled, and gambling on the woman warning him if Dolman attempted to take advantage of his actions, he turned to stroll jauntily away.

Glaring hatred at his tormentor's departing back, Dolman moved his right hand toward the "clamshell" holster. Before he touched the Colt's butt, Marlene stepped in front of him.

"Leave it, damn you!" the woman hissed. "If you don't, I'll warn him. And there won't be any way I can stop him killing you."

"All right," Dolman gritted, accepting the inevitable. "I'll go and make sure there's nothing we can do for Pierre."

"He's dead, and you can leave us to take care of him," Marlene replied, wondering if the Captain also suspected that de Froissart was carrying his copy of the statement. Even if he did, she had no intention of allowing him to gain possession of it. "If I were you, I'd do as Mark says and go back. I don't know how much longer I can keep him from killing you."

"Don't forget that I've left my copy—" Dolman began, wishing that he had done so. If Marlene guessed that it was in his jacket's breast pocket, she would not hesitate to let Mark Counter gun him down.

"What do you think has kept you alive?" Marlene interrupted angrily. "I'll never forgive you for what you did. Mark was right. You didn't give a damn that I might be killed after you'd shot that man."

Looking at the woman's scornful face, Dolman realized that there was no hope of regaining her favor, certainly not as long as Mark Counter was alive. However, the Captain was equally aware of his own danger. If he stayed, and tried to search the Creole, he would be offering the blond giant an opportunity to kill him. Once that happened, they would find his copy of the statement and then they would not even have the anxiety of possible repercussions following the killing of a state policeman.

"All right," Dolman growled. "I'll go, but I'll be coming down to Pilar—"

"You'll always be welcome," Marlene purred, satisfied that she had won.

Letting out a low curse, Dolman swung on his heel and went to pick up his saddle. Waiting until sure that he did not contemplate any treachery, Marlene glanced to where Mark was still talking to the driver. Then she turned and walked toward the valet.

"What'll we do about Massa Pierre, Mrs. Viridian?" the Negro asked. With the possibility of trouble between the white folks, he had wisely refrained from drawing attention to himself. "He's dead."

"We'll take him home for burial," Marlene answered. "Give me everything from his pockets, then get the tarp from the boot and wrap him in it."

Nodding soberly, the valet started to obey. Producing de Froissart's wallet and cigar case, he handed them to the woman. Then he reached inside the jacket and drew out an envelope. Tucking the other two items under her arm, Marlene took it with barely concealed eagerness. Opening the flap, she looked at its contents. A hiss of relief broke from her as she identified the sheet of paper. It was the Creole's copy.

Silently congratulating herself, Marlene became aware that Mark was returning. Before she could stop herself, she was thrusting the envelope hurriedly into her jacket's breast pocket. However, if he noticed her furtive behavior, he made no reference to it. Instead, he set about making preparations for them to leave.

6

HE'S GOT SOME KIND OF HOLD ON YOU

"If you-all don't mind me saying so, seeing's I admire you for it," Mark Counter drawled as he sat at Marlene Viridian's side in the coach, "you never struck me's being the kind of gal who'd let *anybody* do a meanness to her without wanting to have something done back at them."

"I don't understand," the woman replied, moving closer to him.

After having collected his horse, Captain Dolman had asked Marlene for help to remove the dead outlaws. If he had been hoping for her to change her mind, he was disappointed. Showing no sign of relenting, she had ordered the two Negroes to assist him. On his instructions they had carried the corpses behind a clump of bushes on the side of the trail. With that done, scowling bitterly, Dolman had ridden off toward the way station at which they had spent the previous night.

Satisfied that he had confirmed his suspicions and knowing that any further attentions on his part might drive Dolman beyond the limits of endurance, Mark had kept out of the way. Once the Captain had taken his departure, the youngster had helped with the preparations that were being made for the rest of the party to move on.

While the driver had hitched up the team, the valet had removed a sheet of tarpaulin from the boot of the coach. Then he folded up the table and chairs and returned the food, which he had been on the point of serving when the outlaws had arrived, to the picnic hamper. Placing them all in the boot, he had joined the driver and, under Mark's guidance, they had attended to de Froissart's body. Wrapping it in the tarp, they placed it between, and secured it to, the spare front and rear wheels that were carried on the roof of the vehicle.

Mark had saddled his stallion, but Marlene had suggested that he ride with her. Having fastened his reins to the lashings of the boot, he joined her inside the coach. On boarding, he found that she had tossed de Froissart's wallet, cigar case, and, with the exception of one item, other property onto the opposite seat.

Although Mark had not mentioned the matter, he had seen her examining the envelope. Nor had the furtive way in which she had thrust it into her jacket's inside breast pocket escaped his notice. Thinking back to the words Dolman had used to persuade her to intervene, Mark had decided that the contents of the envelope might make interesting reading. Waiting until the coach started moving, he was now trying to satisfy his curiosity and had selected a way that he hoped would avoid arousing her suspicions.

"Dolman came within a lick and a spit of getting you killed," Mark reminded the woman. "Going by the way he dived under the coach after he'd shot that jasper, he knew what he'd touch off and didn't give a damn you might take some of the lead that'd start flying."

"That's true," Marlene conceded bitterly.

"So I figured you'd want him paid back," Mark went on. "Which's why I kept trying to make him draw down on me. That way I could've killed him legal."

Marlene had asked Mark to join her in the coach so that she could strengthen their relationship. Up to de Froissart's death and Dolman's departure, there had never been an opportunity for her to get on the kind of intimate terms she had felt sure would win the big youngster over completely. Listening to his explanation, she concluded that her task was going to be far easier than she had imagined.

"You'd have killed him for my sake?" Marlene asked, pressing herself lightly against the blond giant and looking up into his tanned, handsome face.

"Just say the word and he's wolf bait," Mark assured her. "I can catch up with him before he's gone five miles and be back afore the coach gets in sight of the next way station."

Knowing that Dolman would never forgive her for what had happened, Marlene was tempted to accept Mark's offer. Only the thought of the incriminating documents they had signed held her back. While de Froissart had been carrying his copy, she could not believe that Dolman would take such a chance.

"No, Mark," Marlene said regretfully, after thinking for several seconds. "You mustn't do it."

"Why not? Him being in the state police don't need to worry us. We'll just reckon he must've been bushwhacked by the two owlhoots who got away, should anybody ask us."

"It's not that—" Marlene began.

"Damn it all, Marlene gal!" Mark snorted in well-simulated indignation and made as if to rise. "He came closer than two peas in a pod to getting you killed, and I don't aim to let him get away with it."

"But, Mark—!" the woman said with a gasp, catching hold of his arm.

"The hell with it!" the big blonde growled. "He's got to be paid back!"

"I daren't—can't—won't let you do it!" Marlene insisted, clinging hold even tighter. In her anxiety she had started to speak without thinking and revised her words in an attempt to prevent herself giving too much away. Putting across her right hand, she took hold of his left and went on, "Please, forget it. For my sake."

"All right, if that's how you want it," Mark replied, and

settled back on the seat. "But it sounds to me like he's got some kind of hold on you. One that means you couldn't let me gun him down, no matter what meanness he's done to you."

As he spoke, the big blonde felt Marlene stiffen, and a wary glint came into her eyes.

"I don't know what you mean," she said.

"Way you're acting, he's got a letter or something stashed away that could cause you a whole heap of grief if it fell into the wrong hands," Mark answered.

"How did you guess?" Marlene blurted out, before she could stop herself.

"Like I told you," Mark replied, squeezing her hand in a gentle and reassuring fashion, which also prevented her from drawing it away, "you're not the kind of girl who'd forgive what he'd done. Yet you kept cutting in every time I'd try to rawhide him into drawing. And it wasn't because you was scared *I'd* go under. You *knew* I could take him. So there had to be another reason, and that seemed like the most likely one."

"That's very shrewd of you," Marlene said in praise.

"So he has got a hold over you?" Mark asked.

"Not over *me* personally," Marlene corrected. "You see, he did something for the company and insisted that we, all the owners, sign a statement to say we knew and agreed with what he was going to do. As I'm one of the owners, I had to sign along with the others."

"This here 'something' he did'd likely come close to being what most folks might call busting the law, huh?"

"Well, yes, but—"

"Bad enough to maybe ruin the company was word to get out?"

"It could," Marlene admitted cautiously.

"Then I'm real pleased you stopped me making a blue window in his skull," Mark declared, wondering if the letter he had seen her put into her pocket was de Froissart's copy of the statement. It seemed likely that each of the signatories would have insisted upon retaining one for his, or her, protection.

"Because I sure's hell wouldn't want anything to happen to you."

"Thank you, Mark," Marlene said, looking at him with what she felt sure he would regard as an expression of adoring gratitude.

"Yes, sir," the big blonde went on. "I'll bet that company of yours makes a whole barrel full of money."

"It does," Marlene agreed, thinking back to the impression he had given her in Fort Worth of having extravagant tastes and being eager to acquire wealth by any means. That had been one of the things that had made her decide to cultivate their acquaintance.

"Thing being," Mark continued, "will it keep on coming in once folks start driving their herds to Kansas?"

"There'll be enough ranchers who won't try for us to keep showing a profit," Marlene answered, pleased to have the conversation turned from the subject of the incriminating statement. She also considered that the time had come for her to give him a hint of her plans for the future and the part she hoped he would play in them. "Provided that it doesn't have to be shared too many ways, of course."

"You've got one less way to share it already," Mark commented, glancing at the roof of the coach to emphasize his meaning. "That is unless ole Pierre's left his piece of the company to somebody else."

"He can't do that," Marlene replied, and explained why not.

"So his share has to be split between you-all, huh?" Mark said pensively, thinking of certain aspects during the holdup that had puzzled him. He also saw a way in which, by arousing her suspicions, he might obtain some of the information he was seeking. "Maybe somebody was figuring on having *two* less partners to cut in on the pot."

"*Two* less?" Marlene repeated, looking and sounding puzzled. "I don't follow you!"

Due to the Negro driver's aversion to there being a corpse close behind his back on the roof, he was urging his team along at a fast pace. Rolling at speed over the uneven surface of the trail caused the Abbot & Downing coach to rock and pitch on its thoroughbraces. One jolt, harder than any other so far, nearly dislodged Marlene from her seat. Giving a squeak of alarm, she clung to Mark. Swiftly he curled his left arm around her shoulders, and her free hand passed behind his back. Bracing them both against the vehicle's motions, he waited for her to make the next move. Nestling still closer, she looked at him in a quizzical manner.

"What did you mean, *two* less, Mark?"

"Just what I said. Maybe somebody was figuring on having two partners out of the deal."

"How do you mean?"

"Well, first off, why'd those fellers reckon you'd have money along?"

"We'd hardly be likely to travel with empty pockets," Marlene pointed out, sufficiently interested to put aside her thoughts of taking advantage of them being alone and unobserved.

"Likely not," Mark conceded. "Only they were looking for *you* 'specially. They even asked if you was from the Pilar Hide & Tallow Company before they threw down on you."

"They thought we were carrying the company's payroll," Marlene reminded him. Then she frowned and went on, "But there's no reason why they should have. When we need money, we always have it brought from the Cattlemen's Bank in Houston."

"And yet, from what they said, that's why they'd come looking for you," the big blonde drawled. "On top of that, they was only figuring on finding you and Pierre with the coach."

"What are you getting at?" Marlene demanded, looking perturbed and trying to draw away from him.

"Suppose somebody had gotten word to those owlhoots that you 'n' Pierre'd be taking home the payroll," Mark elaborated, gently but firmly restraining her. "They'd've been madder'n a hoot-owl boiled in dirty water when they couldn't find it. Fact being, that skinny jasper was already hinting's how they'd do meanness to you to get it. Anybody who knew Pierre'd count

on him not just sitting by and letting that happen. And once
they'd gunned him down, they'd not be likely to leave you
alive."

"That's true," Marlene said with a breath.

"In which case," Mark said in the manner of one who had
proved his point, "that'd make *two* less partners when it came
time to cut the company's pot."

"Are you saying one of our partners sent word to those outlaws that Pierre and I would be bringing the payroll, hoping
that they'd kill us both when they couldn't find it?"

"It could be," Mark replied. "Happen things'd've gone the
way they was meant to, everybody would have figured you'd
been killed in the holdup."

Silence fell on the couple for several seconds, disturbed only
by the drumming of the horses' hooves, the creaking of leather,
and the rumbling of the coach's wheels. Mark felt Marlene's
breathing grow heavier, and the expression on her face told him
that she was perturbed by the conversation. Clearly she did not
like the implications of what he had suggested.

"Thing being," the big blonde went on, after allowing her to
digest the information, "which of them did it? My money'd be
on it being either Schweitzer or Profaci."

"Why?" Marlene asked.

"The only other one'd be your husband," Mark explained,
seeing that she was puzzled by his selection. "I know you and
him don't see eye to eye, but he'd have more to lose than either
of them by you being killed."

"How would he?"

"Like you said, you're a partner. As long as you're alive,
there're two full shares coming into your house. With you
dead, one of them would have to be split three ways. Nope. I'm
betting it was one of the others who rigged the deal. Do you
reckon either of them could've sneaked into Fort Worth while
the fair was on?"

Frowning thoughtfully as she considered the big blonde's latest comments, Marlene did not reply immediately. The discussion they were having had confirmed her belief that he was far

from being a naive, easily manipulated youngster. In fact he was proving to be disturbingly intelligent. Not only did he take notice of what he saw and heard, he was capable of drawing shrewd conclusions from them. The way the conversation was going, she did not know if she cared for his ability in that line.

After her experience with Dolman, Marlene felt disinclined to put too much trust in any other potential partner. Particularly one who showed signs of being just as smart and ruthless as the Captain. While Mark could be of considerable use in her plans to gain control of the company, she wanted him in a subordinate capacity. Until all of the incriminating documents had been destroyed, she had no intention of giving him information that he could use to gain a hold over her.

There was one consolation, the woman told herself. While intelligent and shrewd, Mark was not infallible. If he had been, he would never have discounted her husband as a factor; especially on such flimsy grounds. The question was, should she disillusion the youngster on that side of the affair?

After a moment's thought, Marlene decided against doing so. She felt that it would be unwise to mention that Viridian had been at Fort Worth. If the big blonde learned of the visit, he might connect it with Dolman's comments about the murder of Paul Dover and her reference to how the Captain had performed an illegal service for the company. Under the circumstances it would be most undesirable for Mark to possess such knowledge.

"Not without me getting to hear of it," Marlene finally replied, and saw a way in which she would prevent him from considering her husband as a suspect. "We're all so well known in Fort Worth that somebody would have recognized them and mentioned that they were in town."

"Why sure," Mark answered, sounding as if he was convinced by her explanation. "Anyways they wouldn't've needed to come."

"Why not?" Marlene asked, puzzled despite her reservations on the matter.

"Whoever it was'd know what day you'd be starting out for

home, and there's only one way you'd be likely to travel in this coach. That'd be enough for them to tell the owlhoots where to start looking for you."

"Then it might not have been—!" Marlene began.

"Who?" Mark prompted, when she chopped off her incautious words.

Once again Marlene found herself faced with a quandary. She had been trapped into saying more than she intended and could not think of a way out.

At that moment the coach gave another violent lurch and offered her a solution to the dilemma. She took it swiftly. Letting out a well-simulated yelp of alarm, she clutched with added fervor at the big blonde. Her mouth crushed against his, thrusting her tongue between his lips. Nor did she rely upon the kiss alone to distract his attention. Drawing free her left hand, she transferred it to another portion of his anatomy. From what her fingers encountered, she decided that he would prove an even more satisfactory bed partner than either de Froissart or Dolman.

"Oh, Mark!" Marlene sighed as their lips parted. "Do we have to talk right now?"

Although the big blonde guessed what had brought on the display of passion, he controlled his first inclination to draw away. He realized that to continue with his questioning right then would do more harm than good, for she clearly wished to avoid supplying further information.

"Why, Mrs. Viridian, ma'am," Mark lied. "I can sure enough think of things I'd rather be doing than just *talking* to you."

While anything but averse to a flirtation under the right conditions, Mark did not relish the role he was being compelled to play. However, he realized that Marlene's behavior was more mercenary than romantic. She was merely using her voluptuous body as a means of ending a conversation that had grown embarrassing and dangerous. Nor would he be responsible for ruining a satisfactory and happy marriage by yielding to her wishes. From what she had told him, there was no longer any love between herself and her husband. In fact he had every reason to believe that she had already had affairs with Dolman and de Froissart.

More than ever, Mark was convinced that Viridian was responsible for the cold-blooded murder of Paul Dover and, knowing he had done so, Marlene was shielding him. Not out of love or even loyalty, however, but because she was implicated. On top of that, she and her partners had attempted to prevent Goodnight's scheme from gaining acceptance. The fact that it might, probably would, be the economic salvation of Texas had meant nothing to them. Their sole concern had been that the company's best profits would be reduced once the herds started to flow north to Kansas.

Taking all those points into consideration, Mark laid aside his scruples and started to demonstrate how, despite his youth, he possessed a very satisfactory technique for making love.

The big blonde learned one thing in the course of their second embrace. Slipping his right hand under Marlene's jacket, he found that the envelope was no longer in its pocket. Obviously she had removed and hidden it while he was busy with the preparations for resuming the journey. Being aware that any comment on the matter was sure to arouse her suspicions, he kept silent and employed the hand in a way that she found to be most enjoyable.

Harlow Dolman was killed at the same time that Marlene was deciding that she had been correct in her assessment of Mark's superiority to him as a lover.

Despite having covered about five miles, the Captain had still been consumed by bitter rage to the exclusion of everything else. Such was his state of mind that he never so much as glanced at the sloping, fairly open woodland that lined each side of the trail. The idea that he might come into contact with the two outlaws who had escaped did not occur to him. Instead he was engrossed in plotting his revenge upon the woman and the young blonde for the way they had treated him. He had intended to visit Ram Turtle's saloon, a notorious gathering place for criminals of all kinds near Fort Worth, and obtain the services of a man who could open the safe in the factory's office. Once he had Viridian's copies of the statement in his possession, he could set about gaining control without Marlene's assistance. With that point already decided upon, he had been trying to think up a suitable means of obtaining his vengeance.

Flying from among the trees on the right side of the trail, a bullet entered Dolman's back and shattered his spine before he had reached any conclusions on his revenge. The sudden, unexpected agony caused him to wrench at the chestnut gelding's reins as he was slammed sideways from the saddle. Snorting its alarm at such treatment, the high-spirited animal tried to bound forward. However, although Dolman's left foot left its stirrup iron, the right did not, and the pain had caused his hands to clamp tightly onto the reins. With its master's weight dragging on its head and side, the horse swung in a circle instead of bolting.

"Got the bastard!" Widge said enthusiastically, lowering the Enfield rifle that Dog-Ear had refused to use upon their proposed victim. "Grab his hoss!"

While the other outlaw had declined to commit a cold-blooded murder, he did not hesitate to obey his leader's command. Leaving his place of concealment, he sprinted down the slope and onto the trail to catch hold of and restrain Dolman's horse.

After fleeing from their disastrous attempt at the holdup, Widge and Dog-Ear had headed north parallel to the trail until the condition of their horses—far from top-quality animals—compelled them to halt. While resting, they had seen Dolman approaching and Widge had announced that they would take their revenge by killing and robbing him. If the Captain had been more alert, he might have saved his life. The pair had hidden behind a clump of bushes but had left their horses standing in plain view farther up the slope.

"I'll have his guns, seeing's I lost mine," Widge announced, laying down the borrowed Enfield while Dog-Ear liberated Dolman's foot from the stirrup iron and freed the horse's reins.

FLINT
IF HE HAD TO DIE, AT LEAST IT WOULD BE ON HIS TERMS...

Get a taste of the *true* West, beginning with the tale of *FLINT* FREE for 15 Days

Hunted by a relentless hired gun in the lava fields of New Mexico, Flint "*settled down to a duel of wits that might last for weeks...Surprisingly, he found himself filled with zest for the coming trial...So began the strange duel that was to end in the death of one man, perhaps two.*"

If gripping frontier adventures capture your imagination, welcome to The Louis L'Amour Collection! It's a handsome, hardcover series of thrilling sagas by the world's foremost Western authority and author.

Each novel in The Collection is a true-to-life portrait of the Old West, depicted with gritty realism and striking detail. Each is enduringly bound in rich, Sierra-brown leatherette, with padded covers and gold-embossed titles. And each may be examined and enjoyed for 15 days. FREE. You are never under any obligation; so mail the card at right today.

Now in handsome Heritage Editions

Each matching 6" x 9" volume in The Collection is bound in rich Sierra-brown leatherette, with padded covers and embossed gold title... creating an enduring family library of distinction.

SILVER CANYON LOUIS L'AMOUR
THE DAYBREAKERS LOUIS L'AMOUR
FLINT LOUIS L'AMOUR

Without waiting for his companion to concur, the lanky outlaw bent, and tried to twist the Captain's revolver from its
holster. When it did not move, he placed his foot on the body
and gave a harder wrench with both hands. The "clamshell's"
mechanism snapped and its front flapped open.

"Looks like you've busted it," Dog-Ear commented unneces-
sarily, kneeling and reaching inside Dolman's jacket to search
its pockets.

"Yeah!" Widge gritted and thrust the revolver into his own
holster, which had been made to take the larger army Colt.
Ignoring the weapon's bad fit, he looked at the wallet and an
envelope that his companion had brought into view. Only the
former interested him. "That looks fat 'n' full."

"Sure does," Widge conceded, and opened the wallet. The
first thing to meet his gaze was a silver badge pinned to the
inside. Being unobservant by nature, he had never paid any
attention to the insignia worn by members of the state police.
However, while he did not know what kind, he realized that
their victim was a peace officer. "You went 'n' killed a lawman,
Widge!"

"We're *both* in it's deep's each other," Widge warned,
snatching the wallet and staring from it to Dolman. He, too,
failed to identify it, but did not wish his companion to know.
"He's only a Pink-Eye that they'd hired to help guard the payroll."

"Then what's he doing coming back this way?" Dog-Ear
challenged, looking a little less perturbed at hearing that—according to his leader—their victim was an agent of the Pinker-
ton National Detective Agency and not an official peace officer.

"He likely figured's, seeing they'd run us off, the money'd be
safe and he'd head back to Buck Ridge to have the bodies
fetched in case there's bounties on 'em.' Widge guessed and
indicated the envelope that had slipped from the other's fingers.
"What's in that?"

"I dunno," Dog-Ear replied, picking it up and extracting its
contents. "I can't read."

"It ain't nothing important," Widge declared, after studying the statement of Viridian's intentions, without informing the sole survivor of his gang that he, too, was illiterate. He ripped the sheet of paper into fragments and tossed them into the air to be scattered by the breeze. "Hey, though! That means there's only the big feller with the coach."

"Him 'n' the woman," Dog-Ear corrected.

"She don't make no never mind," Widge stated. "They'll stop the night at Joel's Bluff way station. Happen we head down that way, we can catch up with them on the trail tomorrow and have another crack at grabbing the payroll."

"What about him?" Dog-Ear wanted to know, nudging the body with his toe.

"We'll take him a fair piece from the trail and hide him good," Widge replied. "It'll be a long while afore he's missed."

"That big feller's real dangerous," Dog-Ear warned.

"He won't get a chance to be," Widge answered, determined to make another attempt at earning the money offered by "Laxterby" as well as grabbing the payroll. "There's not going to be any riding up and talking this time. We'll drop the big son-of-a-bitch as soon as we see him and keep on shooting until there ain't none of them left alive."

7

HE'S ONE OF RIBAGORZA'S SCOUTS

"Whee-doggie!" Gus Roxterby said enthusiastically, staring with delight at the articles that Constable Hubric brought into the factory's office after having searched the three dead Mexicans preparatory to delivering them to the undertaker in Pilar. "This here's sure our lucky day, Stack."

Considering that the lanky man was being far from tactful in displaying such delight over their good fortune, the corral supervisor made only a noncommittal grunt in reply. Knowing their employer pretty well, Stack Leathers doubted whether he would approve of, or share, Roxterby's pleasure.

Raising his gaze from the cause of the floor supervisor's exclamation, Austin Viridian confirmed Leathers's summation by scowling malevolently.

On hearing the news that had been brought by Otis Twickery —a surly, unclean, generally unpleasant and obnoxious man whose most savory way of earning a living was to hunt wolves for their skins—Leathers had acted in a sensible manner. Returning to the factory, he had instructed Roxterby to remain there instead of taking the bodies into town. Although the floor supervisor had not been too eager to accept the advice on learning what had caused it, he had done so when Leathers had pointed out that Viridian would want it handled that way and on being promised that there would be as little delay as possible in sending help from the town.

However, the burly hide and tallow man's displeasure had not been caused by him believing that Leathers was wrong in giving the advice, or through Roxterby having disobeyed his orders by taking it. The feeling stemmed from another matter. Viridian would never have offered to let the supervisors share the Mexicans' property if he had known that Gomez's pockets would yield close to a hundred dollars, while the other two had been carrying fifteen and eighteen dollars respectively. With both beneficiaries present, he had known that there was no easy way in which he could avoid keeping his promise. Taken with some of the other results of Leathers's arrival at the general store, that knowledge did nothing to improve Viridian's already simmering temper.

Listening to the news that Ribagorza was likely to arrive before there was any hope of them obtaining extra men, Viridian realized that Schweitzer would not give him the money that Roxterby was supposed to be going to use to hire them. On top of that disappointment, there had been his annoyance at having been shown to be in error with his judgment. There had also been threat of very real danger for him to consider.

Without having waited for anybody to suggest it, or asking either partner's permission, Jesse Sparlow had taken it upon himself to organize defensive preparations. He had thrown himself into the task with commendable vigor. In fact there had been times when Viridian had considered that the gambler's zeal had gone beyond that of a mere—if loyal and helpful— senior employee in de Froissart's saloon. It had implied that he believed that he had a sizable stake in the future of the company.

Although Viridian had resented Sparlow's assumption of control and attitude, he had grudgingly conceded—but only to himself—that he could not have done better. The shortage of men raised a number of problems and made it impossible for them to ensure complete protection against the Mexicans. While the company employed a number of Negroes, it had been felt by the partners and Sparlow that to ask them to take part in the defense might establish a dangerous precedent and create difficulties in the future. So, utilizing their limited fighting force to its fullest advantage, the gambler had managed to supply just enough men to defend the factory and yet retain the bare minimum required to patrol the town during the hours of darkness.

It had been while listening to Sparlow quelling the protests of those citizens who had wished to stay and guard their homes instead of going out to the factory that Viridian had had misgivings. Of course, as the gambler had pointed out, the town did depend upon the continued operation of the company for its prosperity and existence. What Viridian had disliked most was the way in which the gambler—whose only connection with the company stemmed from being employed in one of the partners' independent business interests—should have been so determined to ensure that nothing happened to the factory.

There had only been one slight ray of satisfaction for Viridian while all this was going on. Although Sparlow had promised to send two men to guard her, Gianna Profaci had refused to consider spending the night in her home. Taking advantage of the opportunity that was being presented to him, Viridian had suggested that she occupied one of the spare bedrooms at his house. In that way, he had informed Schweitzer, Sparlow, and Leathers, he and his Negro servants would protect her and save using two men who were needed to help with the patrolling of the town. If the speed with which the woman accepted was anything to go by, she was not only aware of, but concurred with, his secondary motive for making the offer.

Having procurred an arrangement that he felt sure would make up for his failure to contact Gianna in the woods, Viridian had gathered the factory's defenders. Although the woman had accompanied them, Sparlow and Schweitzer remained in the town. The former had wanted to continue with his organizing of the patrols and the latter had returned to his store so that he could purchase the wolves' skins that Twickery had brought to sell. Rather than waste a man who would be useful in the work that lay ahead, Viridian had ordered Hubric to come and deal with the three corpses.

On the way to the factory Viridian had told Leathers to go and locate the Mexicans so that they might assess the full extent of the danger. While anything but a coward, the corral supervisor was also no fool. Realizing how much risk would be involved in such an undertaking, he quickly produced sound reasons why carrying it out might be inadvisable. He had pointed out that, according to Twickery—who had no apparent cause to lie—Ribagorza and his men were already behaving as if they were expecting trouble, in which case the precautions would include posting guards or having scouts out when on the move. Leathers had stated frankly that, being aware of the high quality of the men who would be performing those tasks, he did not believe he could approach the main body without being detected. Once that happened, he had concluded, Ribagorza would realize that Gomez had failed and was most likely dead. Then he would suspect that preparations were being made to deal with him on his arrival. Admitting the advantages of preventing their enemies from becoming aware of their readiness to meet an attack for as long as possible, Viridian had countermanded the order.

Telling Roxterby—who had not attempted to conceal his relief at the party's arrival—to have the indoor staff complete their work, then send them to assist the corral hands, Viridian wasted no time in setting about making the preparations. With so few men at his disposal and such a large area to cover, he had seen the wisdom of establishing strong, well-protected defensive positions and meant to have the Negroes construct them. While showing the other white men what he wanted, he sent Hubric to attend to the three dead Mexicans.

In Viridian's absence the bodies had been carried into a lean-to at the end of the office annex. The two horses had been caught and were tied to one of the structure's supporting posts. Showing surprising initiative, Roxterby had had the dead animal taken into the factory so that it could be disposed of in the same way as the slaughtered cattle.

Leaving the rest of the party from the town to attend to the construction of the various defenses, the supervisors had joined their employer and the constable in the office. As Hubric had been watched by both of them, he had not contrived to divert any of the trio's property. While neither Leathers nor Roxterby had envisaged such a windfall, they had felt that it was advisable to keep an eye on the constable and to make their division of the loot as soon as possible.

"Yes, sir," Roxterby went on cheerfully, so engrossed in contemplating the piles of money that he was oblivious to Viridian's obvious displeasure. "This here's turned out a whole heap better'n I thought it'd be. I never figured on getting more'n a couple of dollars cash-money from all three of 'em."

"Or me," Leathers admitted pensively. He had no objection to his opposite number incurring their boss's wrath, but had no intention of duplicating such folly. So he continued by raising a matter that had been puzzling him. "Most of it's pretty near new ten-dollar bills. I wonder where they got 'em from?"

Listening to the corral supervisor's comment, Viridian found that it caused him to reconsider his earlier conclusions regarding the incident. In the first place he had believed that Gomez's attempt on his life had been made on the spur of the moment and had arisen out of a sense of outraged dignity over being dismissed in such a manner. Then, on hearing that Ribagorza was coming, he had wondered if the reason he had given to Schweitzer might have been correct after all. Looking at the money, he decided that the little *segundo* could have had a motive that was not connected with the business he had been sent to handle. Sparlow had claimed to have seen Giuseppe Profaci talking to Gomez in the town of Bryan. If they had been discussing Ribagorza's new policy for dealing with the company, the Italian might have seen a way in it to remove at least one of his partners.

"So do I," Viridian grunted, after several seconds of silent deliberations. He did not offer to take the supervisors into his confidence and discuss his latest theory. "Finish off here. I'm going to see how the work's coming along."

"What'll we do about tomorrow, boss?" Roxterby inquired, grabbing up his pile of money and stuffing it into his pocket.

"How do you mean?" Viridian asked.

"Shall I tell the men to come to work, or stay at home?" the floor supervisor wanted to know.

"There'll still be at least twenty head in the corral, boss," Leathers added. "Happen they're still alive when the shooting starts, they're likely to get spooked and try to bust out. Not that they'd do it, but they'll sure as hell run off some of their tallow."

"I could put them down now, but that'd mean keeping the men inside working most of the night," Viridian growled. "And there's plenty needs doing to get ready for Ribagorza. Don't tell them anything unless they ask. Then say that they'd better be here the same as always in the morning."

"That'd be best, boss," Leathers stated. "If Ribagorza sees them working, he might not guess we're waiting for him. And you can count on them to keep well out of the way once the lead starts flying."

"Yeah," grinned Roxterby. "And if any of 'em should get shot, it'll be making the greasers waste lead and we won't need to pay 'em."

Ignoring the floor supervisor's comment, although he considered that it had a certain amount of merit, Viridian left the office. Looking around, he located Gianna near the factory's main entrance. She was talking to a couple of the defenders, but glanced his way and nodded as he signaled for her to join him.

Feasting his eyes upon the woman as she approached him in her usual hip-swaying, sensual fashion, the hide and tallow man mentally licked his lips in anticipation of how he was hoping to spend at least part of that night. However, having more important and serious matters on his mind, he thrust such thoughts from it. He wondered if Gianna could throw any light upon a couple of the points that had occurred to him while he had been considering the possibility of Profaci having conspired with Gomez to kill him. In addition to that, he wanted to enlist her support in a scheme by which he might turn the trouble with Ribagorza to his advantage.

"Let's take a look around and make sure that everything's being done properly," Viridian suggested as the woman reached him. Taking her by the right arm, without waiting to hear whether she agreed or not, he led her away from the office and went on, "When did Joe decide to go down to Houston?"

"I don't know," Gianna replied. "Why?"

"He never said anything about it on Thursday night when we went to see Bernie and find out what news Pierre had sent from Fort Worth," Viridian explained.

"He hadn't told me he was thinking of going, either," Gianna admitted. "He just came back and told me to pack some clothes in his saddlebags, then went on Friday morning."

"Did he tell you why he was going?"

"Sure. He said he was thinking of making the livery barn bigger and wanted to buy some timber from the sawmill."

"Then he'd likely have a fair amount of money with him," Viridian remarked, half to himself.

While speaking, the burly man had been gazing about him to find out how the work was progressing. If he had been watching the woman, he would have seen that the words had a disturbing effect upon her.

"He did have!" Gianna said, as a frown creased her brow. "I saw him put his wallet into the jacket he was using. It was so thick that he must have been carrying plenty of money."

Noticing the change that had come into the woman's voice, Viridian swung his eyes toward her. He found that she was exhibiting a tight-lipped expression similar to that which Marlene adopted when suspecting that something was wrong. So although the reply had implied that the money had been in bills rather than coins, he decided not to ask any more questions about it for the time being.

"You know, Gianna," he said, wanting to divert her attention. "I've always thought what a pretty widow you'd make."

"Mama mia! How—?" The woman gasped, jerking her arm

free and staring at him with alarm. Then, making an almost visible effort, she regained control of her emotions, and her voice was almost normal as she went on, "Why did you say a thing like that?"

"I was just thinking that it's a pity I didn't know he was going," Viridian replied, wondering what had caused her reaction.

"Did you want him to bring something back for you?" Gianna inquired, starting to walk again and looking to where some of the corral hands were setting up a breastwork of logs.

"No," Viridian answered, taking her arm once more. "It's just that if I'd known, maybe he wouldn't be coming back. Would that have worried you?"

"Not too much," Gianna confessed, turning her face toward him once more.

"And if he didn't come back," Viridian continued, "you and I could see more of each other."

"I don't see how," Gianna stated. "You'd still have Marlene watching you."

"Maybe. Maybe not," Viridian countered. "The way things are these days, with so many outlaws around and all, anything can happen when you're traveling."

"What do you mean?" Gianna demanded, the wary glint returning to her eyes.

"There're always stories in the newspapers about people being killed in holdups," Viridian hinted.

"How did you know—?" Gianna began, stiffening slightly.

"I don't know *anything*!" Viridian interrupted, failing to notice how her question had been worded, although he felt her body tense as it had just before she had pulled her arm free. She did not do so again, and he continued, "There'll only be Marlene and Pierre in the coach, and it's a mighty lonely trail between here and Fort Worth."

"Marlene and Pierre!" Gianna repeated, looking and sounding as if a weight had fallen from her mind. "That's who you— What you mean—"

"I don't *mean* anything," Viridian corrected. His instincts warned him not to mention his hopes regarding Marlene and de Froissart in case the men hired by Roxterby should fail to do their work. "All I said was that you keep hearing about people being killed in holdups."

"Yes," Gianna admitted, studying the burly man with interest, "you do."

"If—and I'm only saying *if*—something bad should happen to Marlene on her way home," Viridian went on, squeezing her arm gently, "I wouldn't be a married man anymore. Would I?"

"No, you wouldn't," Gianna conceded, and her relief was even more obvious. There was a slight pause before she reminded him, "But I'd still be married."

"Maybe something can be done about that," Viridian hinted, so engrossed in putting the woman into the required frame of mind that he did not notice how her comment had appeared to have been an afterthought. "Did Joe tell you how long he'd be in Houston?"

"No."

"So you don't know when he's likely to be coming back?"

"No," Gianna repeated. "I'd think at least a week. Probably more."

"I'll ask Bernie if he knows," Viridian decided. "He might know. Joe stopped with him after I left on Thurs—hellfire! So he did!"

"What's wrong?" Gianna asked as Viridian came to a halt with a scowl on his face and fists clenched.

Reaching a decision, the burly man resumed his walking and told the woman what he suspected. His reason for doing so was simple. The news de Froissart had sent by telegraph on Thursday had been that it was almost certain Goodnight's scheme would be accepted by the majority of the ranchers. Remembering how Profaci had remained with Schweitzer after he had left aroused an unpleasant possibility. Perhaps they had concluded that the company had too many partners.

"Mama mia!" Gianna gasped at the conclusion of his explanation. "You could be right, Austin."

"I think I am," Viridian replied, and considering that the

time was ripe for it, went on, "I agree with them. There are too many partners to share in the profits. Only I've got different ideas about who should go."

"Who?"

"Everybody except you and me."

"Just the two of us," Gianna purred. "That sounds good to me. When do we start?"

"Tonight, with Bernie," Viridian answered, and told her of his plan.

"It could work," Gianna admitted, and he could see that she was excited. "With Bernie gone, there'll only be Marlene and Pierre—and Joe."

"We'll get around to them," Viridian promised, failing to notice that the reference to her husband had again appeared to come as an afterthought. "In fact if everything goes right, there could only be Joe left."

"You mean that you've already made arrangements to get rid of Marlene and Pierre?" Gianna gasped.

"I've done what I could," Viridian answered. "But it might not come off. Don't worry, though. If we miss this time, there'll be other chances."

At that moment Leathers came over from the office. Although the corral supervisor seemed to be strolling in a nonchalant manner, there was an air of tension about him that was plain to Viridian.

"Don't let on you know, or start looking, boss," Leathers advised. "But there's a feller watching us from up on that rim."

"The hell you s—" Viridian began, then glared at Gianna, who had gasped and was on the verge of doing what Leathers had said they should not. "Stand still and don't look. Who is it?"

"I've not seen him too plain," the corral supervisor admitted. "But I'd reckon he's one of Ribagorza's scouts."

'Mama mia!' Gianna yelped, staring about her in consternation as she realized that she was standing exposed and some distance from the nearest shelter. "He might start shooting at us."

"It's not likely, ma'am," Leathers drawled reassuringly. "He's close to half a mile away and'll just be looking us over." Turning his attention to Viridian, he continued, "Trouble is, boss, he'll go back and tell Ribagorza we're getting ready for him."

"Can you stop him?" Viridian inquired.

"I wouldn't count on it," Leathers replied. "He'd see me coming, and when I got to where he is, he wouldn't be there."

"How far off do you think Ribagorza is?" Viridian asked.

"Not all that close, boss," the corral supervisor guessed. "I don't reckon he's near enough to get to us tonight."

"I don't want to count on that," Viridian declared. Seeing how the scout's presence in the vicinity might be turned to his advantage, he threw a glance at the woman to make sure that she understood the significance of what he said next. "What worries me is that when he hears we're ready at the factory, he might hit at the town."

"He might at that," Leathers agreed, before Gianna could speak. "We'd best send word to Jesse Sparlow."

"I'll go and tell him if you like," the woman offered.

"Hubric can do it when he takes the bodies in," Viridian told her. "He's about ready to go."

"I'll go with him," Gianna stated. "The thought of that man watching us makes me shiver. Anyway, in return for you letting me stay at your place tonight, I'll cook you a real Italian supper. That's not a thing I can do in a hurry."

"Now that's an offer I don't intend to miss out on," Viridian conceded with a grin. "You go ahead and do it. I'll be in as soon as I've made sure we can handle Ribagorza if he hits at the factory and not the town."

8

HE WAS IN CAHOOTS WITH RIBAGORZA

"Marlene's been threatening to have the servants throw these out ever since Ribagorza gave them to me," Austin Viridian remarked, indicating the sombrero and poncho that he had donned as a disguise. He had also exchanged the clothing that he had worn at the factory for a dark blue shirt and black trousers, while his Hersome gaiter boots had been replaced by a pair of Kiowa moccasins. Emerging from beneath the poncho, the butt of his Remington showed that he had retained his gunbelt. "It's lucky that she never got around to doing it. If I'm seen, they'll take me for a greaser."

Lying naked in the big double bed, Gianna Profaci nodded sleepily and without too much interest. Faintly, from somewhere downstairs, she heard the chimes of a clock. The time was three in the morning, and Viridian was getting ready to leave for the attempt at removing his senior partner.

It had been close to sundown when Viridian had been satisfied that all the arrangements for defending the factory were completed and had taken his departure. Soon after Gianna had left, Leathers had reported that Ribagorza's scout had also gone. Although the corral supervisor had maintained unceasing vigilance, he had failed to detect any further evidence of them being kept under observation.

On his arrival at Pilar, Viridian found the street cleared and the citizens in a state of readiness. Armed men were gathered at the New Orleans Saloon, and the first group were about to begin their patrol duties. Jesse Sparlow said there had been nothing to suggest that Ribagorza had men watching the town, although he admitted that it was possible they could have done so without being seen.

While approaching the town, Viridian had watched a couple of the saloon's employees dragging a limp, unresisting Otis Twickery across the street to the jail. On his commenting upon the matter, Sparlow explained: Apparently there had been a disagreement over the price offered by Schweitzer for the wolves' skins. Although Twickery had finally accepted, he was clearly dissatisfied and in a bad mood when he arrived at the New Orleans. Knowing that liquor always had an adverse effect upon Twickery's never-too-amiable nature, Sparlow's first inclination had been to refuse to serve him. However, Schweitzer warned him that to do so might be dangerous. If Twickery left town in his state of annoyance, he was capable of finding Ribagorza and telling of all he had seen. Accepting the storekeeper's advice, the gambler had given orders to the bartender. As soon as Twickery had shown signs of growing abusive, a Mickey Finn had been slipped into his drink. It was Sparlow's intention to have the unconscious man held in jail until after the Mexicans had been dealt with.

Having given his approval of the gambler's arrangements regarding Twickery, Viridian had learned all he could about the way the town would be patrolled. By the time Sparlow finished explaining, the burly man felt sure that he could carry out his scheme with a reasonable chance of success.

Despite what Viridian had told the other men at the store, he sent the Negro servants to their homes after they had completed their work. To make sure that the men carrying out the patrol knew he had changed his clothes, he invited them into the mansion for coffee at half past eleven. To emphasize the point, he explained how he considered it was inadvisable to wear a white shirt. If there should be trouble and fighting in the dark, such a garment offered too good a target for safety. He had also requested that they should hold the noise down as Mrs. Profaci was sleeping in the guest room above their heads. With those precautions taken, he had let them out of the kitchen's door. Then he put a can of kerosene and a loaded shotgun by it, so that he could find them without needing to light a lamp when the time came to make his move. Having completed his preparations, he joined Gianna in his and Marlene's bed and they had made love in what he had regarded as a most satisfying fashion.

"Wish me luck," Viridian requested, watching with approval as she left the bed and picked up the nightgown she had discarded when he joined her.

"I do," Gianna assured him. "But I'd better go to the room I should be using so that I'll be there when they come to tell us what's happened."

"Sure," Viridian agreed, eyeing her curvaceous body as it disappeared under the contour-concealing garment. "It's a pity we won't be able to get back together when I come in."

"There'll be plenty of other times," the woman pointed out. "You'd better get going, hadn't you."

"Sure," the burly man repeated, and walked from the room.

Viridian descended to the ground floor. Moving quickly through the pitch blackness, he found his way to the kitchen. There he struck a match so that he could avoid the various obstructions between him and the side door. Shaking out the flame as it drew near to his fingers, he found the key and turned it in the lock. Opening the door, he peered out and listened for a few seconds. Satisfied that nobody was near, he picked up the can of kerosene in his right hand. Collecting the shotgun in his left, he emerged and closed, but did not lock, the door behind him.

Waiting until his vision had grown strong enough for him to form a general idea of where he was going, the burly man set off across the garden. As he did so, he reviewed his plan to make sure that he had not overlooked any major detail. It was basically the same one he had meant to use to avoid having to return the money that should have been advanced by Schweitzer to hire reinforcements. He realized that the presence of Ribagorza's scout in the vicinity would add to its credibility.

By cutting through the woodland instead of using the main driveway, Viridian hoped to avoid the patrolling men and make his way to the rear of Schweitzer's store. Once there, it would be a simple matter to spread the kerosene around and start a fire that would be difficult—if not impossible—to put out. Then, retiring to a place of concealment nearby, he would await developments. If he was lucky, his partner would perish in the conflagration. Should Schweitzer get out, Viridian planned to kill him with the shotgun and rely upon the prevailing confusion to escape after he had done it.

From the first, the burly man had accepted that the scheme involved a fair amount of risk. He also believed that he had managed to reduce it considerably. Nor had he forgotten about Schweitzer's copy of the statement. He knew that it was in the safe at the store, which he would be entitled to open after his partner's death.

Thinking of that aspect reminded Viridian about his wife and de Froissart also having copies. Although that had slipped his mind when—in the heat of his anger—he had given his orders to Roxterby, he was not worried unduly by the omission. He expected that the Creole would have left his copy at the New Orleans Saloon. In which case, if the holdup was successful, Viridian could obtain it in the same manner as Schweitzer's. Should Marlene be carrying hers, it would be returned to him as her next of kin. If not, she would have hidden it in the house and he could search for it at his leisure. He hoped that it would be the latter alternative. There was a chance that it might reach undesirable hands if it was found on her body. Of one thing he felt certain: Neither his wife nor his partners would have taken the kind of precautions that he had threatened to do. Like himself, they would be disinclined to put such an incriminating item into anybody else's possession.

Setting aside his thoughts as he left his property behind, Viridian concentrated on moving as silently as possible and listening for the patrol. The night was fairly dark, but his eyes had grown accustomed to it. He could see well enough to avoid colliding with the trunks of the trees or blundering into the bushes. He did not hear any sounds to suggest that the men on duty were on that side of town, which was as he had hoped it would be.

There was one problem Viridian felt grateful he would not have to contend with. Wishing to avoid false alarms, or disturbances that might lead to panic, Sparlow had requested that everybody who owned a dog would keep it indoors. To the burly man's relief, it appeared that all the citizens had carried out the gambler's instructions.

The tranquillity of the woods was only disturbed by natural night sounds: the call of an owl as it flitted through the trees or other animal noises. Then Viridian thought that he detected a brief rustling of leaves from behind and to his left. Faint though it had been, he turned his head and stared in its direction. Try as he might, he could not see anything to account for it. For all that, he felt uneasy as he started to walk onward.

Stepping even more carefully and lightly, Viridian continually darted looks over his shoulder. He became aware of an eerie sensation of being watched, but failed to discover any evidence to support the belief. After covering about fifty yards, he was approaching the edge of the woodland. Shrugging his shoulders, he told himself that his nerves had been playing tricks on him.

A twig snapped!

Under normal conditions, Viridian would have missed such a faint sound. In his present state of tension, with his ears straining and helped by the silence of his surroundings, it struck him with the impact of a rifle-shot.

Swinging to his left, the burly man saw a shape that was blacker than the surrounding darkness as it moved swiftly toward him. He sensed rather than saw that the figure's right arm was raised, but he knew for sure he was not imagining the brief flicker of something thin and bright in its hand.

Snarling a curse, Viridian took a hurried step to the rear. At the same instant he brought up and flung the can of kerosene at the approaching shape. He had two ideas in mind by doing so: to distract, if not disable, his attacker and to free his right hand for using the shotgun. However, even as he released the can, his retreating foot caught against a protruding root, and he toppled backward.

Releasing the shotgun, due to an instinctive desire to try to break his fall, Viridian landed on the ground. Either the can had missed its mark or it had failed to affect his assailant. Continuing to advance, the man straddled his feet apart and bent so that he could drive home the knife. Desperately Viridian coiled up and thrust out his legs. He felt his feet impact against the man's chest and shoved with all his strength. Nor had he been a moment too soon. Even as his assailant was flung erect and away, the knife hissed around. It barely missed Viridian's chest as its wielder was compelled to retreat rapidly.

Although Viridian had removed the most immediate threat to his life, he knew that he was anything but safe. With that in mind he sent his right hand flashing across to the left. It met only the coarse, blanketlike material of the poncho and could not reach the butt of his Remington.

Either the attacker had lost his knife on being sent staggering or he had guessed what the burly man was trying to do. Whatever the reason, although he had not fallen, he did not attempt to return, despite having reeled backward several steps. Instead there was a rasping of steel being dragged hurriedly across leather and followed by the unmistakable sound of a revolver being brought to full cock.

Rolling rapidly to his left, in a near-frantic attempt to avoid being hit, Viridian passed over the shotgun. Even as he felt its hardness against his ribs, there was a crash of detonating black powder, and he saw the muzzle blast of his attacker's revolver flare briefly but brightly in the darkness. However, his swift movement had achieved its purpose. He felt fragments of earth pattering against the back of the poncho as the bullet plowed into the ground barely three inches behind him.

Halting supine, Viridian scrabbled with his right hand until it found and closed around the wrist of the shotgun's butt. Bending his right leg, he tilted the weapon upward. He used his right knee to support the twin barrels, while the heel of his left hand was occupied with drawing back both hammers simultaneously. As the clicking of his assailant's revolver reached his ears, he squeezed the first and second triggers. With a double roar that merged almost into one sound, the right and left tubes flung out nine buckshot balls apiece.

Dazzled by the violent red glare that belched from the shotgun's muzzles, Viridian was unable to see the result. However, he heard the soggy impacts of the two loads striking flesh. At such close range the balls had not started to spread to any great degree. Caught in the chest by the two groups in rapid succession, the man was flung bodily through the air. His revolver bellowed, but with no greater result than to send a bullet into the branches of a nearby tree. Then he crashed to the ground, but was dead by the time he landed.

Blinking his eyes in an attempt to regain his night vision, Viridian dropped the shotgun. Although he doubted whether it would be needed, he cleared a way to his revolver with his left hand and drew it as he started to rise. For a moment he stood breathing deeply like an enraged bull and glaring at the slightly twitching blob on the ground.

"Stinking greaser bastard!" Viridian spat out, then realized the significance of the yells that he could hear emerging from the town.

Attracted by the sound of shooting, men would be coming very shortly to investigate. Some of them would probably be carrying lanterns. Even if they were not, despite the fact that he had lost the sombrero, his appearance might arouse their suspicions. Certainly they would be puzzled at why he was wearing the poncho. Perhaps one or more of them might even guess what he had been planning to do.

Sure enough, there were lights glinting and swaying among

the buildings. Swiftly the burly man returned his Remington to its holster and snatched the poncho over his head. Muttering curses, he searched with his feet until one of them came into contact with the sombrero. Grabbing it, he looked around for a hiding place. Already he could make out vague shapes behind the lights and knew that he must move fast. Not far away was a clump of bushes. Gliding silently toward them, he thrust the two garments underneath.

"There's somebody!" yelled an excited voice.

"It's me!" Viridian bellowed, guessing that he had been seen and aware of the danger. "Don't shoot!"

"Hold it, damn you!" barked Sparlow's southern drawl. "It's Viridian!"

Under the circumstances the hide and tallow man was willing to forgive the gambler for failing to say *"Mr.* Viridian".

Hurrying forward, the men with the lanterns afforded Viridian his first clear view of the man who had tried to kill him. First the pool of light illuminated a pair of filthy Indian moccasins and leggings. Next he saw yellow-striped, light-blue cavalry breeches, garments such as he had never seen worn by a Mexican. Even though the greasy buckskin shirt had two holes each as large as a teacup in its chest, from which blood was spreading in copious quantities so as to hide any marks of identification, he realized that it was Otis Twickery before the hideously distorted features came into view.

"Hey!" yelped one of the townsmen as the party crowded around. "Look who it is."

"What happened, Mr. Viridian?" another went on, a question that was being put by several more of them.

"Shut up, for God's sake!" Sparlow bellowed, and silence fell. Then he continued in a quieter tone. "What happened, Mr. Viridian?"

"What's this over here?" said a voice.

For a moment Viridian wondered if the speaker had discovered the sombrero and poncho. Then he realized that the voice was coming from the wrong direction for this to be the case.

Turning his head, he watched the stageline's telegraph operator picking up the can he had thrown at his assailant.

"Looks like kerosene," offered one of the saloon's bartenders.

Once again excited comment and queries welled up, to be quelled by Sparlow, who repeated the request for information.

"From the look of it, he was in cahoots with Ribagorza," Viridian answered. "But how the hell did he get out of jail?"

"That's something we'd better find out!" Sparlow said. "I told Hubric to stay there all night."

"Did you think that Twickery might try to escape?" Viridian demanded.

"No. I just didn't want that stupid son-of-a-bitch *you* call a kin—constable underfoot," Sparlow answered, and ignoring the hide and tallow man's angry scowl at the reference to his relationship with Hubric, went on, "Tom. Run to the jail and find out what's happened."

"Yo!" replied the man to whom the order had been directed, giving the traditional cavalry assent to a command, and turned to lope away.

"Hey!" yelped one of the party, staring about him nervously. "If Twickery had help to escape, there might be more of 'em around."

The words caused some consternation as various members of the party considered their implications. There were startled exclamations and numerous worried glances directed at the surrounding darkness, which seemed to have grown suddenly even blacker and more menacing.

"I didn't see or hear any," Viridian stated, not displeased that Sparlow had also overlooked the possibility of Twickery having companions in the vicinity. "But some of you'd best take a look around my place and Profaci's."

"Take three men and do it, Maxie," Sparlow ordered. "If the shooting's woken Mrs. Profaci up, tell her there's no cause for alarm and that Mr. Viridian's not been hurt."

"I know that Otis Twickery wasn't feeling too friendly toward Bernie Schweitzer," the telegraphist commented, after the four men had taken their departure. He was perturbed by the way the party was shrinking and spoke to help keep up his spirits. "But why did he come hunting for you, Mr. Viridian?"

"Maybe Ribagorza paid him to do it," the hide and tallow man replied. "He reckoned they'd met on the trail."

"How'd you come to be out here?" Sparlow wanted to know.

"I thought that I could hear somebody moving around up near the house and went to take a look," Viridian answered, thinking fast. "When I didn't see anybody, I reckoned I'd better come for some men to help me make a more thorough search."

Even as he finished speaking, the hide and tallow man realized that there had been a couple of dubious points in his explanation. While he was trying to think up a logical reason for his being awake enough to hear the noises at such a late hour, or why he had come through the woodland instead of taking the easier route along the driveway, there was a shout from the town. Then, waving his lantern erratically due to the speed at which he was traveling, Tom came racing toward them.

"What's wrong?" Sparlow demanded as the man came up.

"H-Hubric!" was the gasping, almost breathless reply. "He— He's de—dead."

"Dead!" the gambler repeated, displaying far more emotion that was usual for him. "How the hell did it happen?"

"H-he'd been—knifed—in the back," Tom explained. "I—I found him sitting in the chair at his desk. The side door was open, and he was dead."

"The greasers must be fixing to attack the town, not the factory!" the telegraphist squawked, glaring wildly from point to point as if expecting to see Mexicans leaping at him from behind every bush.

"Don't get spooked!" Viridian advised, seeing a way in which he might prevent the ownership of the kerosene being questioned. "I'm betting Ribagorza sent a man in to get Twickery out of jail—"

"How did they know he'd got his-self put in?" a man interrupted.

"They must have had scouts watching the town as well as the

factory," Viridian replied. "Anyways, unless I'm mistaken, the feller who let him out has gone back to the rest of the greasers."

"Why?" Sparlow inquired.

"I think Twickery was supposed to come out here and set fire to either my place or Profaci's," Viridian explained. "That would have drawn everybody away from the town and maybe even from the factory to help put it out. Enough for them to be able to attack without too much danger, anyway, even if you didn't all come."

"You could be right at that," Sparlow declared, then indicated the body. "If you are, they'll have a long wait. But we'd best get the men back to town in case they don't."

Listening to the gambler, Viridian wondered if he might once again inadvertently have guessed correctly regarding the enemy's motives.

9

THEY'VE NEARLY KILLED
YOU TWICE

Even though the Negro driver had been carrying Pierre de Froissart's corpse behind him on the roof of the Pilar Hide & Tallow Company's coach since early the previous afternoon, he had not overcome his superstitious dislike for its presence. So, in order to have it removed as quickly as possible, he was traveling at a fast pace. Not only that, but he had been driving for most of the night and by nine o'clock in the morning was feeling very tired. Consequently he was not watching the trail as carefully as he should in view of the fact that the six horses that were drawing the vehicle were strange to him. To make matters worse, he was approaching an area where vigilance ought to have been his primary concern.

Although the driver did not know it, Mark Counter and not Marlene Viridian was responsible for his lack of sleep.

Having no desire to share a bed with the woman and being aware that she believed that it was possible for them to do so, the blond giant had been equally certain that she would not take kindly to any ordinary refusal. Using considerable tact, he had achieved his purpose without antagonizing her. He had done so by convincing her that he wanted nothing more than to consumate their lovemaking in a way that had not been practical while traveling, but he was willing to forgo the pleasure rather than have it put her in danger.

Mark had begun by mentioning that there were certain disadvantages to spending the night at the Joel's Bluff way station. If they should stay there, he pointed out, de Froissart's body would attract attention. Then they would be expected to telegraph the news of the holdup and its result to Pilar. To do so would warn whoever had hired the outlaws that the affair had been only partially successful. In which case that person might organize another, more effective attempt on her life. Marlene had suggested that Harlow Dolman might send the information from Buck Ridge. Mark had countered this by guessing that after the way they had treated him, the Captain was unlikely to do anything that he would regard as being helpful to them. Much to his relief, she had yielded to his arguments. In fact, such was her ego that she had soon come to consider the decision her own idea.

On reaching the way station shortly before sundown, Marlene had told the driver and de Froissart's Negro valet that they would be continuing the journey as soon as they had eaten a meal. Following Mark's advice, she had also warned them not to mention the holdup or what was wrapped in the tarp on the coach's roof. To make sure that they obeyed and to fend off any undesirable questions, Mark had remained with the men while Marlene had gone to inquire about the possibility of hiring a fresh team.

With the needs of his big bloodbay stallion attended to, and satisfied that the corpse was not the object of interest or speculation, Mark had gone to join Marlene at the way station's main building. As he entered the dining room, he had found her dropping a blazing sheet of paper onto the fire. Although he guessed that it was the one she had received from the Creole's valet, he pretended to accept her explanation that she was destroying a bill for an expensive hat that she had bought but did not want her husband to learn how much it had actually cost.

After they had had a meal and rested for a couple of hours,

the replacement team was hitched to the coach so that they could move on. Once they had started, Marlene insisted upon resuming their interrupted lovemaking. Mark had obliged for a time, until he felt she might be willing to give him information. Then he had pretended to be struck by a disturbing thought. He brought the conversation around to the statement that had prevented him from killing Dolman and suggested that de Froissart might have a copy that could fall into the wrong hands now that he was dead. Wishing to impress him, Marlene replied that—like all partners—the Creole had had one, but that now there was no cause for alarm. After his death she had taken possession of it. In fact he had seen her burning it at the way station. She did not attempt to explain why she had lied about it in the first place and Mark was too wise to press the point.

The night had dragged by with Marlene growing increasingly restless. She was annoyed at being unable to culminate their kissing and caressing as she desired, due to the uncertain motions of the coach. Mark had not been sorry when she had fallen asleep in his arms and had soon joined her. Shortly after dawn the driver halted to rest the horses and they took a cold breakfast. With Marlene in such a surly, unpleasant mood, Mark had decided against trying to obtain any information. They would be in Pilar by noon and he hoped that he would find the answers there.

Yawning tiredly, the driver allowed his borrowed team to pick their way down a fairly gentle slope and across the bed of a dried-up stream. Instead of sticking to the hard-packed center of the trail, they moved over to the right. Just an instant too late he realized what was happening. Yelling an alarmed "Whoa!" he thrust on the brake's handle with his boot and hauled back desperately at the reins.

Being unaccustomed to their new driver, the horses failed to respond quickly enough. They swerved as he had signaled through the reins, but did not obey his command for them to stop. Although the right front wheel just scraped by the large rock that jutted up through the gravel of the stream's bed, the larger rear wheel extended sufficiently to reach it.

Perhaps the wheel would have surmounted the obstacle if it had been turning. Held immobile by the grip of the brake's shoe, it buckled and two spokes were splintered as the vehicle was brought to an abrupt halt.

Instantly pandemonium reigned. Dozing on the box, de Froissart's valet was pitched from it. He landed on the rump of the near-side wheelhorse, causing it to rear and deposit him supine on the ground. More fortunate than his companion, the driver contrived to remain on his seat. Cursing savagely, he fought to prevent the thoroughly alarmed team from trying to bolt.

Inside the coach, Marlene was locked in Mark's arms and kissing him. The abrupt cessation of motion took them both by surprise and threw them from the seat. A screech of fright burst from the woman and she clung tighter to the big blonde. Managing to free his right hand, he thrust it forward. His palm slapped against the upholstered backrest of the front seat, preventing them from crashing into it.

"What's happening?" Marlene shrieked, as they rebounded, still entangled, onto the seat from which they had been thrown.

"I don't know," Mark pointed out, liberating himself from her grasp and coming to his feet. "Stay put while I go and find out."

With that the youngster opened the door of the coach and sprang to the ground. He alighted with hands ready to scoop the matched army Colts from their holsters and eyes darting around. Discovering what had happened, he ignored Marlene as she appeared at the door. Running forward to catch hold of the lead pair's heads, he helped the driver bring the horses under control. With that done, he went back and looked at the damaged wheel. Fastening the reins to the brake handle, the driver jumped from the box and joined him.

"How did *this* happen?" Marlene demanded, glaring furiously at the colored man.

"Well, ma'am," the driver replied. "There was this here rock—"

"Can we fix it, friend?" Mark interrupted before Marlene could say another word.

"Well, sir," the driver answered, scratching his head and looking up the slope down which they had descended. "We've got most everything we need to take that busted wheel off— 'cepting we can't do it."

"Why not?" Marlene barked, climbing down.

"We just ain't got no way of holding the coach up while we changes the wheels, ma'am," the driver explained. "And we can't change 'em unless it is held up."

"Do you mean to say that we're going to be stuck here, with that?" Marlene snapped gesturing toward the roof of the coach.

"Where's Pierre's valet?" Mark asked, having followed the direction indicated by the woman and realizing that a member of their party was missing.

"Damned if I didn't forget him," the driver said. "He done gotten his-self throwed off when we hit that rock."

Followed by Marlene, the two men hurried to the other side of the vehicle. They found the valet, looking disheveled and dazed, trying to rise.

"Are you all right, Joe?" the driver asked, hurrying forward to help the other Negro stand up.

"I reckons I is," the valet decided after testing the movements of his arms and legs. "It's like the Good Book says, the Lord takes care of his own."

"Likely," Mark conceded, guessing that the man's escape from injury had come through him being taken by surprise. So, instead of trying to break his fall, he had landed relaxed rather than tense. "Now let's see what we can do about getting the coach fit to move."

"It'd be easy enough, happen we could get us a long, stout pole, sir," the driver said miserably. "Only there ain't one around. Them bushes hereabouts ain't big enough nor strong enough for us to use 'em."

"The nearest woodland's back at Joel's Bluff, unless Pilar's closer," Mark drawled pensively, thinking about the change in the nature of the terrain. Since they had left the way station, they had been traversing open and rolling range country. For a moment he studied the coach, then tested the consistency of the gravel underfoot with his boot's toe. "Will that wheel hold up long enough for you to get it on to harder ground, do you reckon?"

"Just about, maybe sir," the driver replied dubiously as he measured the distance to what would be the bank of the stream. "It sure won't go much farther."

"That'll be far enough," Mark assured him. "Take it over and unload it."

"What are you going to do, Mark?" Marlene wanted to know.

"See if we can't change the wheel," the blond giant answered. "It's either that or I'll have to ride on to Pilar and fetch help."

"Send Jackson," Marlene suggested, nodding in the driver's direction. "I'm not staying here alone."

"It'd take him too long on one of the team horses," Mark pointed out. "And I don't reckon he could handle my blood-bay."

"I sure enough wouldn't want to try, sir," the driver declared, darting a glance at the big horse which—with its saddle removed and carried on top of the coach—was fastened to the boot as it had been the day before.

"Then we'll have to do what we can here," Mark stated. "Take her over like I said, friend."

"I'd best have the axle nut off first, sir," the driver suggested. "That way, the wheel'll come off when it starts to collapse. If it can't, it'll maybe bend the end of the axle and we'll be in worse trouble."

"Do what you want," Mark authorized, accepting that the man's knowledge exceeded his own in such matters.

"What do you have in mind, Mark?" Marlene inquired as the driver went to the front of the coach, climbed on the wheel, and produced a spanner from the boot under the seat.

."Like I said," the big blonde answered. "See if we can change the wheel."

Without further explanation, Mark watched the driver remove and place the axle's nut in his pocket. Then, climbing aboard his seat, he liberated the reins and released the brake. At the driver's request, Mark went to the lead horses' heads and helped to make the team back up a short distance. Showing considerable skill, the man started them moving forward. Watching until he was satisfied that the rear wheel had passed the rock, he guided them steadily toward the edge of the stream. Although the wheel wobbled and wavered, it did not leave the axle. Nor, due to its sturdy construction and dished shape, did it collapse. However, the men knew that it would never have lasted the remainder of the journey.

Once the vehicle was on solid ground where its wheels did not sink in as they had while crossing the gravel bed of the dried-out stream, Mark set the men to work. While the driver started to unhitch his team, the valet began unloading the boot. Releasing the bloodbay, Mark led it to one side. He removed its bit and reins, leaving on the bridle but allowing the lead rope to dangle and ground-hitch the animal. Climbing onto the coach, he passed down his saddle and the wheels to the waiting men. Next he lowered de Froissart's body into their reluctant hands. That was a task that none of them relished, but it had to be done.

What Mark did next came as a surprise to the other members of the party. Spreading his horse's blanket beneath the wagon, he knelt on it in such a manner that his shoulders were under the rear axle.

"Get ready to take the wheel off, Joe," the big blonde instructed, looking up at the startled faces of his companions. "And you be set to put the other on in its place, Jackson."

"You don't mean you're going to try—?" Marlene began.

"It's that or stay here until somebody comes along to help out," Mark answered, then slowly and deliberately he began to press upward.

At first, to the onlookers at any rate, nothing appeared to be happening. Under the coach, Mark could feel the great weight resting upon his shoulders. It seemed to be as completely immovable as if the rims of the wheels were fastened to the ground. Gritting his teeth, he summoned up every ounce of power in his two-hundred-and-sixteen-pound body and continued to strain with all his might. Perspiration bathed his face, which was set in lines of grim determination and effort. The sleeves of his shirt stretched tight against the expansion of his enormous biceps.

"He can't—" the valet began.

"Look!" commanded the driver, grasping the spokes of the five-foot-one-inch reserve rear wheel tightly as if he hoped that by doing so he would help the blond giant to succeed.

"Lordy lord!" croaked the valet. "It's *moving*!"

Struck silent for probably the first time in her life, Marlene stared in awe and was hardly able to believe the evidence of her eyes. Very, *very* slowly, but undoubtedly, the coach's rear end was beginning to move upward. It rose half an inch, then an inch and so onward until the damaged wheel's buckled rim was clear of the ground. With a space of three inches between them, the movement halted.

"Get it off, Joe!" yelled the driver and, when the other man did not respond immediately, added, *"Quick!"*

Galvanized into motion by his companion's final shouted word, the valet gripped the rim of the damaged wheel and pulled. It held for a moment, then slid slowly and reluctantly away from the axle. Even as he staggered under the weight, Marlene shoved him aside and caused him to drop it. Muttering something under his breath that it was fortunate for him Marlene did not hear, the driver stepped around them with the reserve wheel held upright. Working as fast as he dared, he manipulated the hub against the end of the axle. Finding the hole in the center of the former, he carefully eased it onto the latter and thrust the wheel into place.

At that moment Widge and Dog-Ear appeared on the rim of the slope down which the coach had come.

Like the party they were pursuing, the two outlaws had ridden through most of the night. They had passed the way station at Joel's Bluff as dawn was creeping into the eastern sky. Failing to see the coach, they had concluded that their proposed victims must have made an early start. Instead of paying a visit to learn how far ahead the other party might be, they had pushed on optimistically expecting to catch up at any moment. With that in mind, they had ridden at the best speed their horses could manage. As he had taken Dolman's chestnut gelding in addition to the revolver and Henry rifle, Widge could have traveled faster had he been alone. However, he had declined to do so and, although riding the two animals in relay had held his pace down to that which Dog-Ear's mount was capable of producing.

The two men's optimistic feelings had started to diminish as mile had followed mile without them finding the coach. Taken with the open nature of the terrain through which they were passing, the continued failure was beginning to give even Widge second thoughts regarding the wisdom of his scheme. Each was hoping that the other would suggest quitting as they topped the rim and looked down at the dried-up bed of the stream.

"It's *them*!" Dog-Ear yelled, staring and pointing.

Which proved to be an inadvisable, stupid even, piece of behavior.

Being just as capable of seeing what lay before them, Widge had not needed to have his attention drawn to it. Certainly not in such a fashion. The words had carried over the hundred or so yards that were separating them from their victims. Up to that moment the woman, the two Negroes, and the big cowhand who was crouching under the coach had been unaware of their danger. Don-Ear's shout had alerted them to it.

"Mark!" Marlene screamed. "It's the outlaws!"

"Rush the bastards!" Widge snarled, dropping his right hand to the butt of Dolman's navy Colt.

Remembering what had happened on the previous occasion when his leader had given such a command, Dog-Ear made no attempt to obey. Instead, although Widge kicked the gelding to make it move faster, he stopped his mount and reached for the Enfield rifle in his saddleboot.

Without realizing that he was advancing alone, Widge tried to complete his draw. Badly designed and made from poor quality leather to carry a larger gun, the stiff and awkward holster held the revolver tightly. Snarling curses, he snatched with such vigor that he ripped it free. The attempt was only partially successful. While the Colt left the holster, he had put so much force into the effort that his fingers lost their hold on the smooth rosewood handle and it flew from his grasp.

In one way the loss of the revolver ought to have proved a blessing in disguise. Widge was too far away for it to have been of any use. Deprived of it, he transferred the reins from his left hand to between his teeth and extracted the Henry rifle from its boot. Under the circumstances, it was a far more suitable weapon than a handgun.

Beneath the coach, Mark had become aware of the danger just before Marlene had turned, seen the men, and shouted her warning. Instantly he had started to study the situation and sought for a way out of it. Although he did not know if the wheel was in position, he did not dare to wait until he had asked. Bending his arms and allowing his body to sag, he waited until he felt the tremendous weight removed from him. The moment that the vehicle's downward movement ended, he dived forward.

Unlike Widge, the blond giant realized that the range was too great for a revolver to serve his purpose. However, he, too, had an alternative and more suitable weapon close at hand.

When the valet had unloaded the coach, he had removed Mark's Winchester from the hooks on the wall above the rear seat and had rested it against the big blonde's saddle near items that he had removed from the back boot.

Flinging himself forward, Mark reached ahead. Catching hold of the rifle in both hands, he landed on his stomach with the butt already cradled at his shoulder, and rested his elbows on the ground. He decided that Widge was the greater danger for three reasons. First, during the holdup the lanky man had behaved like the leader of the gang. Second, Dog-Ear had been given the task of holding the other men's horses; which implied that he was regarded as the most useless of them. Last and most important, Widge was drawing a Henry repeater, and that would be a far more dangerous weapon than his companion's single-shot muzzle-loader.

Sighting as best he could, with his chest still heaving from the exertion of lifting and holding the coach, the blond giant squeezed the Winchester's trigger. Instead of hitting Widge, the bullet tore into the chest of Dolman's gelding. Screaming in pain, the animal started to collapse.

To give Widge his due, he responded with considerable speed. Kicking his boots free from the stirrup irons, he quit the stricken gelding's back and contrived to land on his feet. Ignoring his own horse, which had torn its reins free from the other animal's saddlehorn and wheeled away in panic, he reeled onward for a few steps. Recovering his equilibrium, he whipped the rifle back to his shoulder and continued to charge down the slope.

While reloading, Mark glanced at Dog-Ear to find that he was having trouble handling the long rifle due to the movements of his horse. So that still left Widge as the greater threat. Striking the ground close by Mark, a bullet gave emphasis to *that* point. Once again the Winchester was lined and spat. Hit in the head, the lanky outlaw rebounded as if he had run into an invisible wall.

Watching his leader fall, Dog-Ear put aside any notion of trying to finish the robbery. He let the rifle slip from his fingers so that he could use them for holding the reins, which he, too, had grasped in his teeth. With them in his hands, he applied his spurs and guided the horse in a half circle to go back up the slope.

Mark was turning his Winchester toward Dog-Ear. Instead, on seeing that the man was running away, he laid it down and rose.

"Where are you going?" Marlene yelled as the blond giant ran to his horse.

"They've tried to kill *you* twice," Mark replied, grabbing hold of the lead rope and vaulting onto the stallion's bare back. "I aim to find out who's told them to."

While partly true, the youngster had something else in mind. He had recognized Dolman's horse and could guess how it had come into the outlaws' possession. As Widge would be unable to supply the information, he wanted to capture the other man. He hoped that, in addition to learning who had hired them, he would get hold of one of the mysterious statements.

10

TAKE THEM AT HIS PRICE

"Here the greaser bastards come, Mr. Viridian!" Stack
Leathers announced, standing just inside the main entrance to
the Pilar Hide & Tallow Company's factory building and pointing to where a bunch of riders were approaching in a cautious
manner along the trail from the south. "They're acting just like
when I first saw 'em. All ready and set to meet trouble."

"We'll give it to them, if that's what they want!" the burly
hide and tallow man promised and glanced at the tall, blond,
exceptionally handsome young Texan who had arrived with his
wife shortly after noon.

While Viridian did not comment on the matter, he was wondering whether Mark Counter would be the deadly and efficient
gunfighter that Marlene had claimed. If so, he could prove
most useful in helping to deal with Ribagorza's Mexicans.
However, once that was done, he would require very careful
watching. Knowing his wife, Viridian had accurate suspicions
of why she had brought the big youngster with her from Fort
Worth. It might, the hide and tallow man decided, be advisable
to ensure that he did not survive the fighting.

A light rider, for all his size and weight, astride a powerful horse that was in the peak of physical condition, Mark had experienced little difficulty in capturing the fleeing outlaw. On becoming aware that he was being pursued, Dog-Ear had done his best to escape and had managed to stay ahead—although at an ever-decreasing distance—for almost a mile. Then his leg-weary and exhausted horse had given out. Seeing the big, menacing figure bearing down upon him, he had drawn and thrown aside his revolver, yelling that he wished to surrender.

Making the capture had provided Mark with little more than negative information. On being questioned, Dog-Ear declared that he did not know from whom Widge had learned of the payroll that Marlene Viridian and Pierre de Froissart were supposed to have been carrying. Nor had finding out that the gang had been misinformed caused him to change his story. Studying him, Mark concluded that he was too afraid to lie. So the big blonde accepted his assurance that only Widge had seen and talked to the informant.

Dog-Ear had insisted, none too convincingly, that he had not known they would come across the coach again and that he had been unprepared for Widge's decision to attack it. Nor could he offer any satisfactory explanation for why they were in the vicinity. Having had no intention of sharing the money that he was expecting to receive from "Laxterby," Widge had not mentioned the rendezvous on Frog Creek. So Dog-Ear had known nothing about it. In the hope of exculpating himself, he claimed that he had believed their sole reason for coming south had been to confuse any lawmen who might be hunting for them.

On the matter of Dolman's murder, Dog-Ear had been explicit if even less convincing. According to him, he had been absent and attending to the demands of nature at the time that Widge had fired the fatal shot. When emptied, his pockets had yielded the Captain's wallet with the badge removed but holding a fair sum of money. He had tried to convince Mark that Widge had made him accept it so that he would be implicated in the killing while retaining the more valuable horse, saddle, and firearms for himself. Pretending to believe what he was being told, Mark had turned to another matter. Further questioning established that only one document had been found in Dolman's possession and that it was destroyed by Widge, who had claimed that it was of no value.

After having ascertained the approximate whereabouts of Dolman's corpse—so that he could arrange for it to be found and given a formal burial—and taken charge of the Captain's property so that he could return it to the state police detachment at Fort Worth for disposal, Mark had permitted the thoroughly frightened outlaw to ride off. He had been satisfied that Dog-Ear had not killed anybody, but had known that taking him into Pilar would in all probability have resulted in him being hanged. Regarding him as more stupid and easily led astray than vicious, evil, or dangerous, the big blonde could not bring himself to cause Dog-Ear's death in such a manner.

There had been another point in favor of Mark letting the outlaw go free. On being delivered to Pilar, Dog-Ear was almost certain to have mentioned the contents of Dolman's wallet. Although the blond giant intended to return all of the Captain's belongings, he had realized that he could not send the money until after he had completed his assignment. To have done so would have been contrary to the character he was playing and might, probably would, have aroused Marlene's suspicions.

As if fearing that his captor would have a change of heart, Dog-Ear had taken a hurried departure. On rejoining Marlene, Mark found that she had already had the two Negroes start to prepare for resuming their interrupted journey. Having replaced the axle's nut to secure the wheel, the driver was hitching up his team, and the valet had almost finished reloading the coach.

The woman accepted Mark's story of how he had failed to catch Dog-Ear but had returned rather than continue the chase as he had not wanted to leave her alone for too long. Learning about Dolman's death had not caused her any concern, except about the fate of his copy of the statement. Without mentioning what he had been told, Mark used the document as an excuse to search Widge's body and the saddles of the two horses. He had not discovered anything informative and felt even more sure that Dog-Ear had spoken the truth about the "letter" having been torn up and thrown away.

With the abortive search concluded, Mark helped the Negroes to return de Froissart's body to the roof of the coach. Then they fastened the dead outlaw across the saddle of his horse, which had been too tired to stray far after having pulled free from the stricken gelding. While the driver had removed and loaded the dead animals' rig onto the coach, Mark saddled his bloodbay. Earlier, he and Marlene had concluded that he should enter Pilar riding his horse and not sitting in the vehicle with her. So he decided that he might as well make a start at it straight away.

From the moment Mark arrived at the town, he had been conscious of the prevailing atmosphere of tension. He felt sure that the appearance of his party had not caused it, for he had become aware of it before the first of the well-armed citizens they had passed could have seen the two bodies.

Gianna Profaci, Austin Viridian, Schweitzer, and Sparlow had been outside the New Orleans Saloon, along with most of the male white population. Although Mark had studied the reactions of the two partners in particular, he had failed to detect any hint of disappointment that Marlene had survived the holdup. Nor had they displayed more than a casual interest in the dead outlaw.

In explaining what had happened, without mentioning their suspicions, Marlene had introduced Mark and given a flattering —if true—account of his fighting abilities. The big blonde had thought that Viridian did not show the kind of pleasure that might have been expected on learning how he had twice saved Marlene's life. He had also seen Schweitzer, Sparlow, and Gianna looking him over speculatively, although the woman's interest and attitude appeared to be different from that of either man.

However, there had been little discussion about the holdup and even less condolences over the death of de Froissart. Instead, Schweitzer had told the newcomers about the incidents of the previous day and night. He had also suggested that Mark might like to assist the party who were going out to guard the factory. On the blond giant agreeing, Marlene had kept quiet until Gianna had stated that she was going with the defenders. Immediately Marlene had said that she, too, would accompany them. From the way she had been scowling at the Italian woman, Mark guessed that she had noticed the manner in which Gianna was eyeing him and did not intend to let them be together unless she was present. Going by Gianna's mocking smile at Marlene, she had understood the other's motives. Clearly they disliked each other, and Mark wondered if he might be able to turn it to his advantage later on.

One other point had become apparent to the big blonde. Neither Marlene nor her husband had been willing to let Schweitzer remain in town while they went to the factory. When the storekeeper had suggested that he should stay behind and attend to de Froissart's body, they had insisted that he accompany them. Mark guessed that Viridian wanted to prevent his partner from obtaining the Creole's copy of the statement. Probably Marlene's intention had been to stop either of them suspecting that it had already been in her possession and was now destroyed. Whatever their reasons, Sparlow had resolved the issue by offering to deal with the corpses as he had to stay in town and organize its protection. So the storekeeper had grudgingly conceded defeat.

When Mark had reached the factory, he had been impressed by its readiness for fighting off the Mexicans. There were well-protected firing points situated to cover the whole area effectively. A concentrated cross fire could be laid down from them and would render any attack a lethal proposition for the men who were making it.

At Marlene's invitation Mark had joined Gianna, the partners, Roxterby, and herself in the main building. The big blonde had not been given an opportunity to study the place. Almost as soon as they had entered, Leathers—who had been making a scout along the trail—had returned bearing news that the Mexicans were approaching.

The longer Mark studied Ribagorza's party, the more he felt that something was wrong. Certainly they were riding as if they were ready for trouble. However, although he would have expected them to be watching the factory and studying the state of its defenses, their attention appeared to be focused on the other side of the trail. That did not strike him as the correct attitude for men who were contemplating an attack upon such a well-protected location.

"Look!" Roxterby said. "Ribagorza's pushing on ahead of his men."

"Hell, so he is!" Viridian agreed, studying the tall Mexican in the silver-decorated charro clothing who was galloping from among the rest of the party. "What's he doing?"

"I'd say he was coming in to make talk," Mark suggested. "In fact I don't reckon he's fixing to attack you folks at all."

"What makes you think that?" Viridian demanded, as every eye turned to the big blonde.

"I grew up around Mexicans, down in the Big Bend country," Mark replied. "One thing I learned early. They don't take seconds to any man when it comes to fight savvy."

"So?" Viridian challenged, annoyed that his companions were showing such interest in the youngster's comments and hoping to lead him into making a stupid assumption.

"So why are they coming like that?" Mark inquired.

"They're not bringing cattle to sell," Viridian scoffed. "That's for sure."

"And they're not acting like men who're fixing to attack *you*," Mark answered calmly. "They can see that you're ready for them, even if their scout hadn't told them you was doing it. Yet they're headed straight here, right out in the open. You allowed he'd have maybe twenty-five men backing him. I count twenty with him. Even if he hadn't left any to handle the cattle, there's not enough over to be sneaking in while we're watching the rest. Was I asked, I'd say you should let him come in and hear what he has to say."

"He might only be coming to demand the advance payment," Viridian pointed out.

"That's not likely," Mark drawled. "If he figures you gunned down his three men yesterday, he'll know the answer was no and won't have changed. Happen that's all he wants, you can tell him the same. But I don't reckon that's why he's here. And should I be right, it'll be too late to apologize once you've let him be gunned down."

"You mean that he might not have told Gomez to kill the boss?" Leathers asked.

"All I'm saying is that those fellers aren't acting like they're figuring on doing their fighting *toward* the factory," Mark answered. "They're looking *away* from it."

"He's right, damn it!" Schweitzer barked, then raised his voice. "Don't anybody shoot unless you get shot at!"

"Somebody he knows'd best go out and talk to him," Mark suggested. "I'll come along, just to prove that I don't think I've called the play wrong."

"You do that," Viridian agreed when his wife and partner looked at him in a pointed manner. He leaned his rifle against the wall. "Come on."

Setting down his Winchester, Mark accompanied the hide and tallow man from the building. He noticed that Viridian was glancing about to make sure that nobody was showing an inclination to fire at the approaching rider. Side by side, they advanced to meet Ribagorza as he turned from the stagecoach trail.

"Hey, *amigo!*" the Mexican greeted in excellent English, halting his horse and dismounting. "My scout told me that you looked like you was expecting trouble. But his horse went lame and he didn't get back too quick, or I'd have been here sooner."

"What for?" Viridian inquired, too puzzled by the turn of events to put the question more politely.

"To help you. What else?" Ribagorza replied, frowning a little. "We're friends, aren't we?" And anyway if anything happened to you, I'd have to start dealing with that thief down at Quintana."

"But Gomez—," Viridian began, sounding even more baffled by the way in which his visitor was responding to the situation.

"Gomez!" the Mexican interrupted, and his frown deepened into a deeper scowl. "Has that short-grown son-of-a-bitch been around here?"

"Didn't you send him to ask—" Viridian growled, then changed his sentence to avoid any reference to the demand for an advance payment. "See me yesterday?"

"Me? The hell I did! I ran him off in the middle of last week. What was he doing around here?"

"He said you'd sent him to collect some money for a herd you'd be bringing."

"You didn't give it to him, did you?" Ribagorza demanded.

"No," Viridian answered, deciding that to lie would be inadvisable.

"That's what I figured, knowing you," Ribagorza grunted. "So what did he do?"

"Tried to kill me," Viridian replied. "We had to shoot him and his two men."

"Good for you," Ribagorza said enthusiastically, then looked around and returned his gaze to the hide and tallow man with an expression of growing awareness. "Hey! You thought that *I'd* sent him! All this's been done ready for *me!*"

"What'd you've thought and done happen you'd been in Mr. Viridian's place?" Mark put in when the man at his side hesitated instead of replying.

Turning his eyes to examine the speaker more carefully, Ribagorza drew one accurate and several erroneous conclusions. The Mexican decided that despite his youth, the blond giant would be a highly competent fighting man. For him to be dressed and armed so well implied that he had a more lucrative form of employment than was common in the war-impoverished state of Texas. The way in which he wore the matched army Colts suggested what it might be. In fact Ribagorza felt sure that he could guess why the big Texan was present. If he had been hired by the Pilar Hide & Tallow Company, it was *not* to carry out any ordinary, routine task around the factory.

One thing Ribagorza knew for sure. You did not take chances, or act tough, around a young man of that kind.

"I'd have done the same," the Mexican conceded, speaking the truth. Then he scowled and went on, "The lousy little bastard. He could have got a lot of us killed. It's lucky you guessed we weren't coming gunning for you, Austin."

"Sure," Viridian answered, without correcting the other man on the matter of who had made the deduction. "But there was a lot to make us think you might be. Otis Twickery told us that he'd passed you on the trail and you looked like you were expecting trouble of some kind."

"I was," Ribagorza admitted. "Gomez swore he'd get back at me when I kicked him out. So we were watching for him in case he managed to get enough help to come back."

"Then if you weren't after us, why did—," Viridian began, becoming aware of what the Mexican's explanation implied. He chopped off the words and changed the subject "I thought that Gomez was your *segundo*?"

"He was," Ribagorza agreed. "Only he'd been getting too big for his breeches. So I sent for my cousin Pepe from Chihuahua to take over, and when he came, I told Gomez he was through. He didn't like it and I had to lay a quirt across his face when he tried to throw down on me. I should have killed him, but you know how kindhearted I am."

"I've seen it," Viridian answered, although to Mark it seemed that his voice lacked conviction. Nor did it change as he went on. "Anyway, he's dead, no harm's been done, and everything's fine."

Which, as the blond giant knew just as well as the hide and tallow man, was far from being correct. While Gomez might have had no other motive than to make trouble for his former *patrón*, that did not explain how Twickery had escaped from jail or why he had apparently been going to try to kill Viridian.

Having watched the meeting proceeding amicably, Marlene, Gianna, and Schweitzer decided that Mark's assumption was correct. So, not wishing to miss anything, they left the factory and went to join the three men.

"Sure *amigo,* everything's *bueno,*" Ribagorza was saying as they arrived. "So I'll send my boys back to fetch the herd—if you want it."

"Of course we want it," Viridian replied, eyeing the Mexican with a wary and suspicious expression. "We've always taken them before."

"Sure, amigo," Ribagorza admitted. "But this's a special herd. It's worth four dollars a head."

"*Four* dollars!" Viridian barked. "You've never had more than *one.*"

"That was different, amigo," the Mexican explained. "Not one of this herd's branded, which makes them *mine.*"

Glancing at Viridian, Mark could see that he understood the comment. An unbranded longhorn belonged to whoever had it in his possession. The youngster also read a second implication in the words. Clearly the Pilar Hide & Tallow Company had been buying what they had known was stolen stock from Ribagorza.

"We went to the trouble of gathering them, instead of just picking up everything we could find," Ribagorza went on, after a brief pause to let Viridian think over what he had said. "So, seeing that they're legally mine, I reckon I should get the legal price for them."

"*All* of them are unbranded?" Schweitzer queried.

"Every last one of the five hundred, *señor,*" Ribagorza confirmed.

"Austin," the storekeeper said, looking at the burly man. "I think Señor Ribagorza's right. We should take them at his price."

"Huh?" Viridian grunted, staring in amazement at his partner.

"They're his cattle, so it's only right he gets four dollars a head," Schweitzer declared.

"Four dollars it is, then," Viridian declared, sounding as if he could hardly believe what he had heard.

"*Bueno,*" Ribagorza grinned, although he, too, showed that he was surprised to have been granted the increased payment.

He nodded to where his men were approaching the track that connected the factory to the stagecoach trail. "We'll go and fetch them. They'll be here by sundown."

"What's the idea?" Viridian demanded, after the Mexicans had taken their departure. "We could have got them for half that."

"They'll be worth every cent of it," Schweitzer replied. "Those ranchers who Marlene's invited are going to go away convinced that Goodnight and his bunch don't believe driving herds of cattle to Kansas is possible."

"What's going to make them think that?"

"We'll have all the cattle Ribagorza brings in branded with Hardin's OD Connected."

"How will that help?" Viridian asked.

"Hardin's backing is what helped Goodnight to persuade the other ranchers," the storekeeper pointed out. "So we'll show them a fake contract that says he'll supply us with a thousand head of either his or Goodnight's cattle a month."

"And that'll make them think Hardin and Goodnight don't really believe driving to Kansas can be done," Viridian went on, nodding approvingly. "That ought to make them all the more eager to sign up."

"It'll do more than that," Schweitzer declared. "Once the story gets around, other ranchers who had believed them are going to change their minds. We'll hint that Hardin and Goodnight are hoping to corner the hide and tallow market by getting everybody else to try to take herds to Kansas."

Listening to the conversation, Mark felt a surge of anger and only by an effort kept it under control. He realized that Schweitzer's scheme could work. Once such a story began to circulate, Ole Devil's political enemies would ensure that it was spread as far as possible so as to damage his reputation for integrity.

"By God, Bernie!" Viridian said enthusiastically. "You've come up with a beauty."

"Give me the keys to the safe in the office and I'll make out the contract," the storekeeper offered. "I can do it while you're having the men start work on the clearing up around here."

"I'll come and help you, Bernie," Marlene suggested, just a shade too quickly.

"No!" Viridian barked, with greater vehemence than such a simple request appeared to warrant. "There'll be plenty of time to do that later. Right now, we'd better go and attend to Pierre's affairs."

Watching the way in which Marlene and Schweitzer were eyeing Viridian in a mutually speculative manner, Mark made a shrewd guess at what had been behind the storekeeper's offer and her suggestion. Clearly Viridian had some objection to his wife and partner opening the safe in his absence. There could be only one reason for that. It held something he did not want them to see.

Mark had already concluded that Viridian and not Dolman had been responsible for the production of the statements and had wondered how the hide and tallow man had disposed of his copy. From what he had just heard and seen, he decided that it must be in the safe. However, unless he was mistaken, Marlene and Schweitzer had respectively drawn the same conclusion.

Everything now depended upon which of them could find a way to lay hands upon the document first.

11
PIERRE MADE ME HIS PARTNER

"Come on in, gentlemen. And may I ask your ladies to join us on this occasion?" Jesse Sparlow said in greeting as Mark Counter, the Viridians, Gianna Profaci, and Schweitzer came to a stop in front of the New Orleans Saloon. "I've set up drinks on the house, so I hope that you'll all do me the honor of joining me."

On seeing that the meeting with Ribagorza had come to an amicable end, one of the townsmen had taken to his horse and dashed into Pilar without waiting for orders. Going by the various sounds which were coming from inside the saloon, the good news was already being celebrated. Glancing at his two male companions, Mark could see that they did not care for what they were hearing.

Schweitzer had not pressed further with the subject of preparing the contracts in the factory's office, which Mark had regarded as a sign that he made it merely to test a theory. Instead the storekeeper had said that he would go back to town. Once again, the Viridians had displayed their reluctance over the thought of him separating from them. Having told the supervisors to have the various defenses dismantled, Viridian had stated that he would accompany his partner. As an excuse for leaving the factory, he had claimed that he wanted to hear more about the two attempts that had been made upon his wife's life.

While Marlene, Gianna, and Schweitzer had shared the buckboard in which they had made the journey out to the factory, Mark and Viridian had ridden their horses on either side of it. The Italian woman had started to praise the blond giant for having been smart enough to deduce that the Mexicans were not coming to attack them. Immediately Marlene had interposed with a question about the death of Dolman and had succeeded in having his attention occupied by answering her all the way to Pilar. It had been obvious to Mark—and the rest of the party—that Marlene had no intention of allowing Gianna to get on too familiar terms with him.

Dismounting, Mark and Viridian left their horses at the hitching rail. On going to help the woman from the buckboard, the big blonde tactfully left Viridian to attend to Marlene. Taking Mark's offered hand, Gianna deliberately contrived to stumble into his arms as she dropped to the ground. He was compelled to catch and hold her against him.

"My, you're strong," Gianna purred, making no attempt to free herself from his grasp. "I hope I didn't hurt you?"

"Shucks, no, ma'am," Mark replied, conscious of Marlene's cold, disapproving gaze. He continued to hold Gianna while darting a glance at the other men. Although Schweitzer appeared disinterested, Viridian matched his wife's expression. So, to a lesser degree, did Sparlow, until his face returned to being its usual impassive mask. The change came so quickly that Mark could not be sure that he had seen correctly. Easing the woman away, he went on. "A dainty little thing like you wouldn't hurt more than a peach blossom."

"Shall we go inside?" Marlene demanded in a voice that was cold enough to form icicles. "By the way, Austin, I've invited Mark to stay with us until the other ranchers arrive."

"I could always bed down at the rooming house," Mark suggested, throwing a conspiratorial glance at Gianna, which he felt sure would bring the required response.

"There's no point in you doing that," Viridian growled, having noticed the glance and—as Mark had hoped—deciding that he would be able to keep a close watch upon the big blonde and Gianna by agreeing to have him stay. "We've rooms to spare and will be pleased to have you stay with us."

"I hope you get the same bedroom I used last night, Mark," Gianna commented. "It was *very* comfortable. Of course you didn't know that I was at your house last night, did you, Marlene?"

"We thought it'd be best, with Joe away," Viridian explained, and took his wife's arm. "Let's go inside."

Mark looked around as they entered the saloon and were being escorted to a table by Sparlow. Clearly de Froissart had been lavish in his spending when building and equipping the place. Although no longer new, the furnishings and fittings were more what would be found in the wealthy section of a major city. However, his thoughts on the subject were brought to an abrupt end.

"Sit down, please," Sparlow said, in the manner of host in his own home. "I'll have anything you want brought over. Keep the drinks going, behind the bar. It's on the house today."

"Just a moment, Mr. Sparlow," Schweitzer snapped, without sitting down.

The gambler had turned and started to walk away while addressing the order to the bartender. At the storekeeper's words, he swung around to face the partners.

"Yes?" he said, and Mark could detect an alert air about him.

"Why are *you* giving away drinks like this?" Schweitzer demanded, and Viridian grunted his agreement.

"It's traditional for the new owner of a saloon to give drinks on the house when he takes over," Sparlow replied, and slapped his left hand against his thigh in what appeared to be an idle, casual gesture.

"We know that," Viridian growled, glancing around with his

main attention on the men at the bar. They were clearly making the most of the gambler's generosity. "But you should have waited—"

The words died away as the hide and tallow man saw three of the saloon's employees converging on Sparlow. Mark, too, had noticed them while studying the barroom, because they had not been drinking or doing any work. Instead they had appeared to be watching the gambler. Apparently that innocent-seeming slap on the thigh had been a signal to them. Although they neither spoke nor came right up to Sparlow, they hovered in the immediate background exuding an air of readiness and menace.

"Why should I wait?" the gambler inquired in a challenging fashion. "Pierre made me his partner just before he left for Fort Worth. *I'm* the new owner."

"He never told *us* about it!" Schweitzer grumbled.

"I thought he had," Sparlow answered. "We were half brothers, and he asked me to join him. Then, if I showed him that I could handle the saloon, he would make me his partner."

"Neither of you ever mentioned you were related," Schweitzer pointed out.

"We didn't want anybody to know," Sparlow countered. "The staff would have figured they had to do what I told them if they'd known I was the boss's brother."

"Nobody's doubting you-all, Mr. Sparlow," Mark put in quietly, watching the gambler and the trio behind him. "And even if they did, you've likely got something in writing to show them they're wrong."

"I haven't," the gambler admitted, in a flat tone that still held a note of warning. "Pierre gave me his word on it. That's all two southern gentlemen need."

"I was with 'em when he gave it," the largest of the saloon trio put in, with the air of proving a point.

Scowling at the speaker, Viridian decided that he would have been more impressed if the confirmation had not been given by a man who had arrived with the gambler. However, the hide and tallow man did not air his misgivings. To have done so would be regarded as casting doubts on Sparlow's and his supporter's veracity.

Basically what the gambler was claiming could have happened. In the past, deals had been made and partnerships formed in the South—involving properties of far greater value than the saloon—with nothing more than verbal agreements to back them. De Froissart had always boasted that he was a southern gentleman, born and raised in Dixie's stern moral code. However, he had always insisted that any business dealing with the other members of the company be put into writing, signed, and witnessed. Of course he *might* have behaved differently with another southerner, especially one of his kinfolk. Sparlow's swarthy features could mean that he had Creole blood. So the relationship was possible, and he had given a valid reason for them not having mentioned it.

"He couldn't have made you a partner in *our* company," Schweitzer protested, while his partner was considering the implications. "That was one of the rules we made when we formed it. We all signed an agreement that each partner's share must revert to the others on his death and couldn't be given to anybody else."

"That's a mighty convenient agreement," Sparlow replied, "for the ones who are left."

"It was all legal and aboveboard," Viridian put in hurriedly, remembering that—despite the trouble they had been expecting —the storekeeper was following his usual habit of not wearing a gun. He also knew that in the event of a showdown, the saloon workers would concentrate upon the armed members of the opposition, himself and Mark Counter, first. "Do you know where the key for Pierre's safe might be?"

"Sure," the gambler replied. "He left it with me. Why do *you* want it?"

"There should be a copy of the company's charter in it," Schweitzer answered for his partner.

Viridian darted a glance at the storekeeper. Like him, the burly man was hoping to find de Froissart's copy of the statement in the safe. From all appearances, Schweitzer was sharing his anxiety over the possibility of Sparlow having read it.

"If it is, I haven't seen it," the gambler stated. "But there's a document box I haven't been—don't have a key to open."

"I may have it," Marlene put in, opening her vanity bag. "There was a bunch of keys among the other things Pierre's valet asked me to look after."

"Can we try them, Mr. Sparlow?" Viridian inquired, hating to be making a request instead of giving an order. "If one works, we can clear things up."

"It's only his share in the company that he couldn't dispose of," Schweitzer went on. "The saloon was his personal property and has nothing to do with us."

Before answering, Sparlow looked around the room. He discovered, as he had expected, that the conversation was attracting attention. All drinking had ceased as the men at the bar watched and listened to what was going on. Then he returned his gaze to the two partners. He knew that everybody was waiting to hear how he replied.

Knowing that he had only three supporters, Sparlow was not ready to force the issue any farther. He was aware that he had no claim to membership of the Pilar Hide & Tallow Company. In fact, he was bluffing about his relationship and partnership with de Froissart. He had merely been trying to find out how Viridian and Schweitzer would react to the suggestion that, due to the Creole's death, he was now the owner of the saloon. Apparently they were willing to accept him in that capacity. So there was no point in bringing about a showdown. Particularly as he felt sure that the majority of the citizens and all but three of the saloon's employees would stand by the partners.

"Come and show me the agreement," Sparlow offered, accepting the keys and other property from Marlene. "If none of these work, we'll break open the lock. It'll have to be done anyway so that I can see what's inside."

"Most likely there'll be some other papers belonging to the company," Viridian remarked, trying to sound matter-of-fact.

"You won't mind us taking them, will you? They're of no value except to us."

"Just *papers*?" Sparlow inquired, and the two words were redolent of suspicion.

"Just records of a few old deals the company's made," Viridian answered, worried by the tone that had entered the gambler's voice.

"There wouldn't be any of the *company's* money in it?" asked Sparlow.

"Of course not," Viridian confirmed, seeing what had caused the questions. "Any money that's there belongs to the saloon. It's nothing to do with us."

"Then you can go and take whatever you find that belongs to you," the gambler promised.

"Some of the papers are confidential," Schweitzer warned. "And, seeing that you aren't a partner—"

"The saloon's all I'm interested in," Sparlow assured him. "You can take all the papers that belong to your company and welcome. Shall we go and see to it?"

"They don't need us, Mark," Gianna commented, sitting at the table to which they had been escorted. She slapped the chair next to her and smiled invitingly at the big blonde. "Come and tell me all about the county fair."

"Why, sure," Mark agreed. "It's between these gents anyway and no concern of mine."

"I'll stay too," Marlene stated and saw the partners throw puzzled looks at her. "It won't need three of us to bring the papers from the safe."

Although Marlene had meant to go with the men, she did not intend to leave Mark and Gianna together. The decision to stay had not been difficult to reach. All along, her failure to mention that she had already destroyed the Creole's copy had been caused by nothing more than malicious pleasure at seeing her husband worried over the possibility of it falling into the wrong hands.

Ignoring the interest she had aroused between Viridian and Schweitzer, Marlene swept around to take the chair that Gi-

anna had offered to Mark. Throwing a triumphant look at the
other woman, she sat down. For a moment, as the other men
walked away, the big blonde was tempted to go and sit at the
other side of Gianna. He decided against doing it. To arouse
Marlene's jealousy might make her more forthcoming, but it
could easily have just the opposite effect. So sitting down with
her between him and the Italian woman, he spent the time that
the other men were away describing—with frequent interrup-
tions from Marlene—the various items of interest that had occurred at the county fair. All in all, he was not very sorry when
the partners and Sparlow returned. He was starting to feel like
a choice piece of meat between two cats.

Studying Viridian and Schweitzer as they stalked toward the
table, Mark decided that they looked perturbed and suspicious.
Strolling alongside them, Sparlow had a typical gambler's lack
of expression, and there was nothing to be read on his swarthy
face. The big blonde knew, without needing to think hard, what
was on the partners' minds. Having failed to find de Froissart's
copy of the statement, each of them was wondering where it
could be.

A thought occurred to the blond giant as he was considering
the cause of the two men's perturbation. Having a safe available, where it could be watched over by a person he had trusted
well enough to make a full partner in his business, why had de
Froissart thought it necessary to take the incriminating document with him to Fort Worth?

Before Mark could draw any conclusion on the intriguing
question, Viridian, Schweitzer, and Sparlow reached the table.
Looking around quickly, Mark found that the gambler's three
supporters were watching. They had withdrawn to their original positions after the partners and their employer had gone to
the office, but did not appear to have joined in the festivities.

"Did you get *all* of the company's papers, Austin?" Marlene
inquired, and Mark could detect the mocking note in her voice.

So could Viridian and Schweitzer, the big blonde decided as
he watched the suspicious scowls that came to their faces and
the way in which they stared hard at her.

"Yes," Viridian gritted.

"Are *you* satisfied, Mr. Sparlow?" Marlene went on, realizing that she had made a mistake and turning her gaze to the gambler.

"I never thought to doubt your husband and Mr. Schweitzer, ma'am. Especially as they've taken my word that I was Pierre's partner," Sparlow replied. "There's only one thing more to be settled, gentlemen, then we can take a drink to his memory."

"What would that be?" Viridian demanded, flickering a gaze that located the new owner's three supporters.

"The town needs a new constable," Sparlow pointed out. "And if you're so minded, I'll take it on."

"*You?*" Schweitzer asked.

As mayor, the storekeeper knew that it would fall upon him to replace Hubric. However, he had not given the matter any thought, and having a solution offered from such a source came as a surprise.

"Why not?" the gambler countered. "Running the saloon's not going to take up so much of my time that I couldn't handle it. There's not that much work involved in being constable either. And most that there is gets caused in here anyway."

"The pay's not high," Schweitzer warned.

"That doesn't worry me," Sparlow declared, but continued as he saw the expression on the storekeeper's face. "Although I won't do it for free. The thing is, I feel something should be done, and without delay, to find out how Twickery managed to escape and kill Hubric."

"So do I!" Viridian stated, and for once he spoke with complete sincerity. Now that he knew that Ribagorza was not involved, he shared the gambler's desire to learn who had helped Twickery escape. "I reckon we should take Mr. Sparlow's offer, Bernie."

"All right," Schweitzer grunted, showing no great enthusiasm. "I'll swear you in tomorrow morning, Mr. Sparlow."

"Tomorrow will suit me fine," the gambler confirmed cheerfully, waving to the table. "Now how about sitting down and taking a drink to Pierre's memory and to my success in both my new ventures?"

Having noticed the storekeeper's thinly veiled reluctance, Mark wondered what the others were making of it. Studying the Viridians and Sparlow, he decided that none of them were attaching any significance or importance to it. On recollecting Marlene's comments at various times during their acquaintance, regarding the storekeeper's parsimony, the big blonde concluded that they were putting it down to his aversion to parting with money under any circumstances.

"We'd like you to make finding out what did happen with Twickery your first chore, Mr. Sparlow," Viridian requested after a waiter had collected their orders and the party was seated around the table. "Don't you agree, Bernie?"

"Yes," Schweitzer confirmed, but without excessive eagerness. "But I expect it will turn out that he tricked Hubric, not that he had outside help."

"That's possible," Sparlow admitted, and turned toward Marlene. "I don't like to suggest this, seeing as he was your kin, Mrs. Viridian, but he might have bribed Hubric to turn him loose, then killed him to avoid having to pay."

"That could be it!" Schweitzer declared, with more vigor than he had previously been showing. Then he, too, glanced in an apologetic manner at the frowning brunette. "I'm sorry, Marlene, him being your kin and all, but—well—"

"That's all right, Bernie," Marlene gritted, more annoyed by the mocking way in which Gianna was eyeing her than for any other reason. "He wasn't close kin, and I know he was far from perfect."

"What I don't see is why he went after Mr. Viridian once he'd got out," Mark commented. "Way I heard it, he was riled because he reckoned he'd been cheated on those wolf skins he'd brought in—"

"I paid him a fair price!" Schweitzer protested, while Marlene darted a grateful smile at the big blonde for having changed the subject.

"Nobody's gainsaying it, sir," Mark drawled. "Only, him

being riled at you, I'd've expected him to have gone after your scalp. Especially after he'd gone to the trouble of getting hold of a can of kerosene so's he could burn you out."

"Maybe that's what he meant to do," the storekeeper suggested. "But he changed his mind when he found there were four men with shotguns covering the store."

"Four men!" Viridian said in a startled voice. Then, realizing that such a display of emotion was likely to attract unwanted attention, managed to continue in an almost natural tone, "Which four men?"

"I got to thinking during the evening that, as Ribagorza wouldn't be able to hit at the factory the way it was guarded, he might come into town," Sparlow explained, showing no sign of noticing how the hide and tallow man had reacted to Schweitzer's comment. "And figuring that the store was owned by the company, it could be his main target. So I had Silky and three more men with shotguns positioned where they could see every side, even in the dark. They had orders to cut loose at *anybody* who went near it."

"That was right smart figuring," Mark praised. "Only it doesn't tell us why Twickery went after Mr. Viridian."

"Probably because he was determined to get back at the company and decided to settle for burning down one of its houses," Sparlow suggested. "What do you think, Mr. Viridian?"

"Huh?" grunted the burly man, jolted from his reverie by being addressed. His face showed the worry by considering the implications of what he had just heard. If he had not been intercepted by Twickery, he would have walked into the trap that the gambler had laid without informing him. "I think we should do everything we can to find out who helped that son-of-a-bitch escape—and why he did it."

12

THERE'S GOING TO BE ANOTHER HOLDUP

Keno! Promenade to your seats!
Hurry up, gals, now don't be slow!
Kiss the poor ole caller afore you go!

Accompanied by a flourish from the musicians—a pianist, a fiddler, and a guitar player—the caller brought to an end the spirited Virginia reel, and the dancers streamed away from the cleared section of the New Orleans Saloon's barroom. For once, the "good" ladies of the town were present and, despite their earlier misgivings regarding the propriety of holding a celebration so soon after de Froissart's death, all appeared to be having a good time.

Giving a graceful bow to the plump wife of the stageline's telegraphist, who was clearly delighted at having been the partner of the most handsome man in the room, Mark Counter ignored the inviting glances that were being directed at him by Marlene Viridian and Gianna Profaci. Fortunately for him, as the wives of partners in the Pilar Hide & Tallow Company, they were both in demand by the other ladies of the town, who only rarely had the privilege of meeting them socially. Several of the townswomen descended upon the pair, who had each taken care to dress her best for the occasion, and Mark took the opportunity to stroll across to the bar.

Although he was the blond giant's host, Austin Viridian made no attempt to greet him as he approached. Instead the hide and tallow man pretended to be absorbed in listening to the livery barn's hostler and the owner of the rooming house as they explained their theories regarding Twickery's escape. Neither of them were coming anywhere close to what Viridian believed had happened, but he found them a convenient way of avoiding the company of the young Texan. Sensing that he was being snubbed, without caring about it, Mark made his way to the other end of the bar. He found an empty space and leaned with his left elbow resting on the bar.

"Enjoying yourself, Mr. Counter?" Jesse Sparlow inquired, joining the blond giant as the bartender slid a schooner of beer to him.

"Why, sure," Mark confirmed, and nodded toward the center of the barroom. "But I never expected to see all these folks here."

"There was some talk that we shouldn't throw a wingding with Pierre only just planted at sundown," the gambler admitted. "But I pointed out that it's a tradition down home in New Orleans to give the departed a rousing send-off and how he'd've wanted it that way."

"Folks sure took you at your word," Mark commented. "But, way they're all drinking like it's going out of fashion, seeing's it's for free, it'll cost you plenty."

"I'll get it back from them in the long run," Sparlow declared confidently. "It's a pity that Ribagorza and his men didn't come in after they'd delivered the herd. I'd've got most of their money from them."

"They went off to see if they could round up some more cattle," Mark pointed out, which was true as far as it went.

On the Mexicans bringing their herd to the factory, Viridian —who had insisted on taking Mark with him—had made an offer to Ribagorza. With Schweitzer's approval, he had prom-

ised to pay four dollars for every head of cattle they could bring
in before the end of the week. The only stipulation had been
that the animals must bear the OD Connected's brand so that
they could be used in the partners' scheme to discredit General
Hardin and Colonel Goodnight. Accepting, Ribagorza had set
off immediately instead of visiting the town for a celebration.

"It's probably as well. I couldn't have made them buy their
drinks when I'm giving it to the white folks," Sparlow said
philosophically. Then, after looking at the nearest men, he lowered his voice and went on, "How do you think Twickery got
out of jail?"

"I don't know enough about it to decide," Mark answered
cagily.

"You asked some pretty shrewd questions this afternoon,"
Sparlow protested. "And I got the feeling there was more than
one who didn't want them answered."

There had only been a little more discussion about Twickery's escape before the party had separated. Although Mark
had tried to keep it going, Viridian and Schweitzer had clearly
been against continuing. Viridian had used the expected arrival
of Ribagorza and the cattle as an excuse to leave, and Schweitzer had claimed that he was wanted at his store.

To Mark's way of thinking, apart from the partners' respective reluctance to having a thorough examination of the matter,
the most significant point had been Viridian's interest in the
guard on the store. He had remarked that the members of the
patrol whom he had supplied with coffee had not mentioned it.
To which Sparlow had replied that, as he had not reached the
decision until almost midnight, they had not known what was
to be done. Mark had formed a pretty accurate conclusion of
what had happened, or should have, but had kept it to himself.

Having finished the drinks and accepted the gambler's invitation to the festivities that evening, the party had gone their
separate ways. Although Marlene had hinted that Mark should
have accompanied her home, Viridian had requested that he go
out to the factory. During the ride Viridian had not been com-
municative. With the cattle purchased, they had returned to the

hide and tallow man's mansion, where they had bathed and made ready for the celebration. Then, after an excellent meal—which Gianna had attended—they had made their way back to the saloon.

"Somebody helped him escape," Sparlow continued when Mark offered no comment. "And it wasn't Ribagorza's men. So who do *you* think it might have been?"

"How would I know?" Mark replied, succeeding in his attempt to sound disinterested. Nodding to where a clearly bored Gianna was still held in conversation with the townswomen, he continued, "Now that's what I call a right fetching woman."

"And a married one," the gambler warned coldly.

"That don't make no never-mind to me," Mark declared in a brash manner, deciding that he had been correct about Sparlow's reaction when Gianna had stumbled into his arms from the buckboard. "Husbands aren't immortal, which'd make her a rich widow should he happen to die. I've always had me a yen for rich widows."

"What makes you think her husband might die?" Sparlow demanded, adopting the flat and emotionless tone that was a professional gambler's stock-in-trade.

"Your—half brother—got gunned down in a holdup, by fellers who was after a payroll there was no reason for them to think he'd be carrying," Mark explained. "And, way things look, somebody's tried twice to get good old Austin killed. I'd say it's getting right unhealthy around here—for some folks."

"You mean that Gomez and Twickery—" Sparlow began, having noticed the slight hesitation when the big blonde had mentioned his relationship with de Froissart. It implied doubt about them being half brothers.

"Shucks, tonight's for funning, not figuring," Mark interrupted, and finished his beer with a long pull. "Looks like the band's going to start up. I reckon I'll see if I can get in the same set* as Gianna."

"I thought you was here with Marlene," the gambler com-

* *Set:* "four couples facing each other in a square formation."

mented, setting down his glass and stepping away from the counter at Mark's side.

"She's got her husband along," the blond giant pointed out, and delivered a conspiratorial wink at the other man. "Which same, a feller should do like a wise old Injun once said, have more than one string to his bow."

Ignoring the scowl directed at him by the gambler, Mark strolled across the floor and asked if he could join the set for the next dance. He saw that Viridian had also quit the bar and was approaching. When the music commenced, the set consisted of Gianna, Marlene, two townsmen, Mark, Sparlow, Viridian, and the local blacksmith. Having moved faster than Marlene, the Italian woman formed a couple with the blond giant. Until the caller organized a general change of partners, Mark was subjected to cold glares by three people.

"What's the idea with *her*?" Marlene hissed, through lips that held what she hoped would pass for a smile of pleasure, as she and Mark twirled around after being brought together.

"Just this," the big Texan replied, no louder. "If I can learn when her man's coming back, there's going to be another 'holdup.' "

"Oh!" Marlene said with a breath, and he felt her relax a trifle.

For all her apparent acceptance of the excuse, Marlene clearly did not intend to let Mark spend too much time in her rival's company. As soon as the dance was over, she made no repetition of her earlier attempts to avoid the townswomen. Instead she started talking to the pair who had shared the set with her. Before Gianna could try to reach the big blonde, who had been coupled with one of the older women during the last stage, Marlene began to praise her cooking. So Gianna found herself being bombarded with questions about recipes.

"I reckon I'd best start to circulate and make sure everybody's got all they want," Sparlow remarked, hardly troubling to hide his satisfaction as he watched Marlene ensnare Gianna. "See you around, gents."

"I don't like to talk business at a time like this, Herb," Viridian informed the blacksmith, giving no sign of realizing that Mark was close by. "But I'd like you to tend to the coach first thing in the morning. Come and have a drink while I tell you what wants doing."

"Well . . ." the blacksmith began, looking at the big blonde in embarrassment.

"You go ahead, gents," Mark drawled cheerfully. "I don't take to business-talk anytime. And anyways, I've got to go out back."

On his return, after visiting the backhouse and relieving himself, Mark strolled across the room. Before he reached the bar, the largest of Sparlow's three supporters came slouching toward him. There was something in the burly man's attitude and expression that gave the big youngster a warning of his intentions. While he did not appear to be armed, Silky's right hand was grasping something in the pocket of his jacket.

Wanting to test his theory and, if possible, avoid trouble, Mark changed direction slightly. He was sure that his summation had been correct when Silky moved to converge with him. Stepping aside at the last moment, Mark deftly averted the collision and, as though he had suspected nothing, walked on without a backward glance. However, he continued to keep an eye on the man via the long bar mirror. Although Silky glared over his shoulder, he did not attempt to follow. Instead he joined his two companions. Noticing how they glanced at him when Silky addressed them, he deduced that he was the topic of their conversation.

Ordering another schooner of beer, Mark watched the bartender until it had been drawn and delivered. If, as he suspected, the incident with Silky had arisen out of Sparlow's desire to prevent him from furthering his acquaintance with Gianna, other precautions could have been taken. Remembering how Twickery had been dealt with in the saloon, Mark had no intention of suffering a similar fate. However, he did not detect anything to suggest that his drink had been tampered with, and he sipped at it while waiting for the next dance.

When the caller requested the formation of sets, Mark set

aside his schooner and walked toward Gianna. Throwing out a challenging glare, Silky cut in front of him. Although the man laid himself open for reprisals, Mark knew that it was not the time to take action. Without making it obvious, he turned aside and asked a woman in an adjacent set if they could make a couple.

Twice during the dance Silky attempted to bump into Mark as they passed each other. Fast on his feet, the big youngster avoided him on both occasions. The incidents made him all the more certain that the saloon worker was trying to provoke him. Mark also concluded that while hefty and probably a skilled brawler, Silky was neither agile nor quick-thinking. Dealing with him did not appear to present any exceptional difficulties, as long as Mark chose the place and means correctly. However, there were his two companions to be taken into consideration. They were hovering in the background, both tall, lean, and hard-looking, with revolvers holstered on their thighs.

Contriving to be some distance away from Silky when the dance ended, Mark returned to the bar. Facing it, he leaned his elbows on top, and his right hand grasped the handle of the full schooner that was placed before him. Instead of drinking, he watched the reflections of the three hard-cases as they approached him. When they came to a halt a few feet to his rear, he guessed that they were determined to force the issue. Standing ahead of his companions, Silky once more had his right hand in his pocket.

"There's one thing I can't stand, Shem, Dub," the big saloon worker announced in carrying tones. "And that's a feller's pretends to be something he ain't. Especially when he's a dude who tries to look like a cow-nurse."

There were a number of men at the counter, and all but Mark looked at the speaker. Silence dropped over them as they realized the words could only apply to the blond youngster. Showing no signs that he had heard, Mark never moved nor spoke. Quickly he scanned the room, with the aid of the mirror, finding—as he had expected—that Sparlow appeared to have left. That figured. The gambler would need an excuse for failing to prevent his employees from picking the fight.

"Hey, boy!" Silky went on, staring at Mark so that there could be no doubt as to whom the words were being directed at. "Are you a dude?"

"Do you mean me?" Mark inquired mildly, without turning.

"Everybody else at the bar's a *man,*" Silky answered. "So it has to be *you*'s I'm talking to."

"Well, now," Mark drawled. "I couldn't rightly come out and say I'm a dude."

"You look hellish fancy dressed for a cow-nurse," Silky pointed out, wanting to plant the idea of an alternative occupation in his audience's head. One that would let him explain the way in which he planned to handle the affair.

"Feller I buy my clothes off'd be right pleasured to hear you say that," the big blonde declared.

Becoming aware of the situation that was developing at the bar, the other occupants of the room fell silent. Through the mirror Mark could see that every eye was turning his way. While Marlene looked worried, neither she nor anybody else offered to intervene. Several of the townsmen appeared to be glancing at Viridian and Schweitzer as if in search of guidance. When none was forthcoming from either source, they stood still and awaited developments.

"That being," Silky continued, raising his voice. He was puzzled by the lack of response and disappointed that his intended victim did not turn or make any other movement that would justify what he was meaning to do. "Cow-nurses don't make enough money to buy fancy clothes like your'n."

There was movement at the bars, but Mark did not make it. While the men nearest to him began to edge away, so as to be out of the line of fire if shooting started, he continued to stand with his back to the trio. From all appearances he might not have known they were there, but he kept them under constant observation.

"You-all figure he ain't a cow-nurse, Silky?" Shem inquired from the left, guessing what his companion was trying to do.

"That's just what I figure," the burly man agreed. "I reckon he's a hired gun, or worse."

"What'd be worse'n a hired gun, Silky?" Dub wanted to know, playing along with the line Shem had taken.

"I ain't sure," the burly man admitted. "But we've got the feller here's can tell us. And he's going to. You heard me, you big son-of-a-bitch. Turn ar—!"

While speaking, Silky advanced and began to raise the Remington Double Derringer without trying to extract it from his jacket's pocket. Such a method of shooting was not conducive to accuracy, and he wanted to be so close that he could not miss. As he started to move, he hoped that the blond youngster would be provoked into turning. If he did not, Silky might find it difficult to explain why he had opened fire.

Silky's hope materialized—but not in the manner he had envisaged.

Timing his movements perfectly, Mark acted with devastating speed. Turning, he jerked up the schooner to propel its contents into Silky's face and brought to an end the shouted request. The abrupt change from apparently passive immobility to sudden and rapid motion took the saloon worker completely by surprise. Temporarily blinded by the flood of beer, he skidded to a halt.

Down and around whipped Mark's right hand, smashing the base of the schooner against the lining of the outthrust jacket at the point where the fist and weapon formed a bulge. There was the crash of detonating powder, mingling with Silky's yelp of pain. Flame spurted through the cloth, which started to smolder, but the .41-caliber bullet found its billet in the front of the bar and not human flesh.

Releasing the schooner, Mark knotted and flung out his left hand. Traveling around and up, with all the weight of his powerful young body behind it, the blow took Silky just above the belt buckle. It plowed inward through his hard muscles as if they were so much soaking newspaper until it seemed to be thrusting his stomach into his chest cavity. Never had the burly saloon worker experienced such nauseating pain, but it did not last for long. Expelling all the air from the lungs in a tormented cry, he doubled forward involuntarily and retreated a couple of steps. Just far enough, in fact, to receive the full benefit of Mark's follow-up to the punch. Moving with lightning-fast precision, Mark brought his right knee to meet the descending face. Once again Silky's torso changed direction. Snapped erect by the impact, he plunged helplessly in his companions' direction.

Although they had been ready to support Silky, neither Shem nor Dub had expected they would need to do so. That they were seeing him being defeated failed to penetrate their heads straight away. Then, as he hurtled toward them, they started to reach for their guns. Blundering backward, Silky scraped between them, and there was insufficient room for him to pass. While he did not hit either man hard enough to knock him staggering, both were thrown off balance. Having disturbed their equilibrium to the detriment of them completing their draws, Silky landed rump-first. Continuing its rearward motion, his torso drove the base of his skull with a crash against the floor. Halted by it, he lay motionless.

Once again Silky's companions tried to fetch out their weapons. Gliding forward fast, Mark shot out his hands. He laid the right against the side of Shem's head and duplicated the movement on Dub with his left. Before either man could resist, he brought their skulls together. There was a click, like two enormous billiard balls making a cannon, and looking as if they had been boned, the pair collapsed limply on being released.

"Behind you, Mark!" Marlene screamed, pointing to emphasize her meaning.

Pivoting around, the big blonde saw the bartender moving along the counter. Even as the man started to reach for something that was underneath it, Mark's right hand dipped, and the ivory-handled army Colt flowed from his off-side holster.

"Bring them out!" Mark commanded, lining the barrel as the hammer clicked to the rear and his forefinger curled across the trigger, just under a second after the hand first started to move.

"And if they come up holding anything except nothing, you'll be dead."

"Easy, friend!" the bartender yelped, staring into the Colt's unwavering muzzle and trying to decide whether it was one or two inches across. He not only obeyed but extended his hand palms outward to shoulder level. "I was only after a wiping cloth."

"Things're never what they look like," Mark commiserated, watching in the mirror for any suggestion of hostility on the part of the other saloon workers.

The door to the owner's private office flew open, and Sparlow emerged on the run. Turning from the bar, Mark swung the Colt's barrel in his direction. Skidding to a halt, the gambler stared at the big blonde. Then his gaze dropped to the three motionless figures on the floor and lifted once more to Mark.

"What's been going on?" Sparlow demanded.

"Unlikely as it'd seem, with my sweet nature, those boys of your'n didn't take to me," Mark replied, trying without any success to read the gambler's thoughts. True he looked surprised, but that would have been his reaction even if he had not ordered the trio to make the attack. Twirling the Colt back into its holster almost as rapidly as he had drawn it, he continued, "Got so demanding that I figured they'd best be cooled down a mite."

"Mark had no other choice but to defend himself!" Marlene put in, wanting to prevent her husband—or anybody else— from using the incident as an excuse to make the big blonde leave town. "Those three provoked and insulted him. The big one even tried to kill him."

"He sure did," the telegraphist confirmed, seeing a way to ingratiate himself with an influential member of the community. There was a general rumble of agreement from the other citizens, and he went on, "Silky was figuring to shoot the young feller and'd done it if he hadn't got stopped."

"The damned drunken idiot!" Sparlow growled, in either genuine or well-simulated anger. "I've never known him to get liquored without looking for a fight and should've watched him, but I was busy." He looked around and went on in a milder, more apologetic tone, "I'm sorry that this happened, folks."

"Shucks," Mark drawled, wondering if he might have been allowing his imagination to run away with him. "There wasn't no harm done, except to them and they'll be no worse than sore-headed comes morning. I'm willing to say it's over and done with."

13

COME OUT WITH YOUR HANDS EMPTY

"You look like a man with more than hunting on his mind, Jesse," Mark Counter commented as, at half past eight on Wednesday morning, he and the gambler were approaching the small stream that flowed through the woods to the east side of Pilar.

"You might say that," Sparlow answered.

"Anything I can help on?" Mark inquired. "You treated me so decent over the trouble with those boys of yours that I'd be pleased to pay you back some way."

"I'm obliged, Mark," the gambler declared, cradling a Henry rifle across the left sleeve of the brown leather jacket he was wearing along with Nankeen trousers and moccasins instead of his normal working attire. "In fact it's the boys I was thinking about."

"Huh-huh," Mark grunted, with just a hint of suspicion on the noncommittal sound.

"Don't worry," Sparlow said hurriedly. "I've seen them this morning. They're a mite sore, but I've warned them that they'd best stay clear of you from now on."

"Reckon they'll do it?"

"If they want to stay working for me—and healthy. Which I don't reckon they will, happen they go after you again."

"You can bet your last red cent on that," Mark stated flatly. "The big feller's luckier'n any one man's the right to be. I don't usually deal that lenient with a man who tries to turn a sneaky gun on me."

"Nobody'd expect you to be," Sparlow replied, and paused as if trying to make a decision, then continued, "And maybe— just *maybe,* mind—*somebody* last night was counting on you not being."

"I don't follow your drift," Mark stated truthfully.

"Those boys've been with me for a fair spell, and I'd hate to lose any of them," Sparlow elaborated. "Especially Silky. He's the only proof I've got that Pierre made me his partner."

"And you reckon's how *somebody* might've given him the idea of jumping me, hoping I'd shoot all three of them down?"

"Not all three. You'd get Silky for sure, maybe one of the others. But the one you didn't stop would cut *you* down."

"This *somebody* wouldn't have a name," Mark growled, and his grasp tightened on the Winchester he was carrying, "now would he?"

"This puts me in one hell of a position," Sparlow grumbled. "I've no proof of anything, and it could've been no more than barroom conversation . . ."

"But?" Mark prompted.

"I've said this much, so I may as well tell it all to you," the gambler decided with every evidence of reluctance. "When I was talking to Silky, I asked him why he'd picked on you."

"You said he always hunted trouble when he'd been drinking," Mark pointed out.

"Sure. And that's all I thought it was until he told me that Austin Viridian had said you was a hired gun."

"Would that've meant something special to him?"

"You bet it would. Of course, Viridian *might* not have known—"

"What about?" Mark demanded.

"Silky's got a real bad hate for hired guns, ever since a bunch of them killed his folks," the gambler explained. "But, like I said, Viridian *might* not have known about it; although Silky doesn't make a secret of it."

By that time they had reached the edge of the stream at a point where it could be crossed by using a series of stepping-stones. Looking back as he was about to go over, Sparlow found that Mark had halted and was glaring in the direction of the Viridians' mansion.

"I reckon I'd best just drift on over and ask good old Austin if he *did* know!" Mark rumbled in tones redolent of menace and suspicion.

"Hold hard!" Sparlow said, sounding alarmed as he grabbed Mark's arm. "That won't get you anywhere. If he did know and meant for you to lock horns with Silky, he'll lie. And if he didn't, he'll guess I've told you. Then he could pretend to believe I'm trying to make trouble for him, which'll give him and Schweitzer an excuse to call in the law."

"How do you mean?" Mark wanted to know.

"Learning that I'm the owner of the New Orleans doesn't sit easy with them, no matter that they pretended to agree," Sparlow explained. "They'd like an excuse to ease me out and, even with Harlow Dolman dead, they've still got too many friends in the state police for me to be able to buck them."

"Why'd you have to buck them?" Mark asked. "Pierre made you his partner in the saloon, even if he couldn't take you one of the company."

"Only verbally," Sparlow pointed out. "They've got *written* proof he was their partner. It doesn't say the saloon's a separate business, but there's no mention of it not being part of the company's property either."

"So you're saying I should just forget it, huh?" Mark growled indignantly.

"No," Sparlow corrected, removing his hand from the big blonde's sleeve. "I'm just saying there *could* be nothing in it. Austin *might* not have known how Silky feels—."

"That's a powerful *could* and *might,*" Mark interrupted, then looked at the gambler and relaxed. "It'd make things bad for you, huh?"

"Worse than I can handle until the lawyer I've sent for comes and has the New Orleans signed over to me legally," Sparlow replied. "He'll be here by Friday at the latest. Wait until that's done and I'll back you up against Viridian."

"You've got a deal," Mark declared. "Just so long as I get to find the truth about him. But I sure hope he doesn't tromp on my toes, or I could change my mind. Come on. Time's a-wasting. Let's go after those son-of-a-bitching deer and I'll call the first mangy old buck I drop Austin."

"That'd be a good name for it," Sparlow conceded and led the way across the stones.

"This's your neck of the woods," the blond giant announced, looking around after completing the crossing. "Where do you reckon they'll be lying up?"

"Could be anywhere between the water and the rim up there," Sparlow replied. "I'd say the best way for us to do it would be to separate. I'll go up and work my way along the ridge, and you follow the stream."

"Seems like a smart way of doing it," Mark conceded. "If I spook them up, you'll get them, and I can take any that you send down this way. Where'll we meet up again."

"I can't stay out for too long, seeing's how I'm being sworn in as constable this morning," the gambler warned, and studied his surroundings in a thoughtful manner. "I'll tell you what. There's a big old silver maple about half a mile down the stream. You can't miss it, there's not another one hereabouts. If we haven't stirred anything up by then, I'll have to call it a day. So I'll meet you at it. We'll be back of Viridian's place and could drop by to see if there's a cup of coffee."

"Now that sounds like a right smart li'l old idea," Mark said in praise. "Austin'll've gone to the factory, and maybe Marlene'll be able to answer some questions for me."

"Maybe," Sparlow grunted. "Well, let's get started. Good luck."

"And to you," Mark said cheerfully. "I'll see you at the maple."

Nodding, Sparlow started to walk up the slope. There was a puzzled expression on Mark's face as he watched the gambler go. The big blonde wondered what to make of the information he had been given.

Certainly there had been no tangible evidence to support Mark's assumption the previous night that Sparlow had arranged for the attack to be made on him. In fact the gambler's whole attitude, after his first understandable surprise, had appeared to be one of contrition over the incident having taken place. Having repeated his apologies to Mark and his guests, he had ordered some of the saloon workers to remove the unconscious trio. Then, promising to deal with them in the morning, he had asked the musicians to start playing.

With the festivities resumed, Sparlow had gone out of his way to make amends to the big blonde. There had no longer been any suggestion of jealousy where Gianna was concerned, although the cause for it had not arisen. Marlene had countered every attempt Mark and the Italian woman had made to get together. After a time Mark had stopped trying rather than chance antagonizing Marlene. Instead he had joined a group of men whom Sparlow had been entertaining with stories of gambling on Mississippi riverboats. Later the talk had turned to deer hunting. Learning that Mark enjoyed the sport, Sparlow had suggested that they go out together the following morning to see if they could bag one of the big white-tailed bucks that were to be found in the woodland behind the town. Despite the fact that he was still harboring suspicions about the gambler, the blond giant had agreed and they had arranged to meet outside the saloon at eight o'clock.

On the way home after the dance Mark had tried to find out what his host, hostess, and Gianna Profaci had thought of the incident. Apparently, if any of them had regarded it as being anything more than Silky's drunken desire to cause trouble, they had been unwilling to say so.

Although Marlene—without any show of eagerness or enthusiasm—backed up her invitation for Gianna to spend the night with them, she had declined. So they had taken her to her home and, to Marlene's ill-concealed satisfaction, had left her at the front door. With that done, Mark and the Viridians had gone on to their own mansion. At no time that night, nor at breakfast, had Marlene been granted an opportunity for a private discussion with the big blonde.

After Sparlow had disappeared among the foliage and undergrowth of the slope, Mark turned in a downstream direction. As he started to walk, he thought about the gambler's information. While he could not remember having seen Viridian in conversation with Silky, there had been numerous occasions when they could have done so without him having become aware of the fact. He realized that Viridian had a stronger reason than Sparlow for wanting him out of the way. While the gambler might have been jealous, Viridian probably suspected why Marlene had invited Mark to visit Pilar.

Sending Silky after Mark would have appealed to the hide and tallow man for two reasons. First, he hoped to remove a serious threat to his life. Second, if he had been fortunate, he might also get rid of the only person who could prove Sparlow's claim to ownership of the New Orleans Saloon. With Silky dead, there was a better than fair chance that the business would fall into the hands of de Froissart's established partners.

One of the points Mark regarded as damning evidence of Sparlow's participation could have been discounted if he had spoken the truth. Silky would have waited until his boss was absent from the barroom before attempting to pick a fight with a potentially influential visitor.

"One thing's for sure," Mark told himself silently, working the Winchester's lever to feed a bullet into its chamber. "Standing here thinking's not going to solve anything. There'll be time to start doing that after I've finished hunting."

The big blonde had not been exaggerating when he had told Sparlow how he enjoyed the sport in which he was now participating. One of his favorite outdoor pastimes was matching his wits and skills against a wary white-tailed deer. So he thrust all thoughts of the attack from his head, being determined to make the most of his period in the woods and away from the people who controlled the Pilar Hide & Tallow Company.

Studying the terrain, Mark decided that the deer would be among the bushes rather than out in the open. He based his decision upon knowing that *Odocoileus Virginianus Texanus,* the Texas variety of white-tailed deer, was a ruminant. As such, it was capable of consuming a large quantity of food in a short time to be stored in its paunch and later, having retired to a place of concealment, chewing its cud. Unless he was mistaken, any deer so close to human habitation would have done its feeding during the night and was now lying hidden.

With that in mind, Mark did not stay close to the edge of the stream. Instead he ascended the slope a short distance and, moving with great caution, traveled parallel to it. Wanting to locate the deer rather than scare it from its hiding place and toward Sparlow, he advanced from cover to cover, continually scanning every inch of the terrain ahead of him.

Despite his caution and careful scrutiny, Mark failed to locate a deer. In fact he soon became aware that he was not even seeing old traces of their presence. There should have been evidence in the form of tracks, droppings, or bushes from which they had cropped leaves and twigs while feeding, but he found none.

The farther Mark went, the greater grew his puzzlement over the lack of signs. Even if Sparlow had known that the deer were likely to be lying up at the rim, and thus had selected the most likely area in which to hunt, there should have been traces of them down by the river.

"Damn it all!" Mark mused as he found himself scanning his surroundings for something a damned sight more dangerous than a buck white-tailed deer. "This chore's getting me as jumpy as a blind man trying to pick a rope out of a nest of rattlesnakes. I'll be starting to mistrust *me* next."

For all that sentiment, the big blonde continued to move with —if anything—even greater care. Yet nothing happened, and the woods seemed to be completely devoid of life. At last he saw the furrowed and scaly grayish trunk of a tree with large, deeply lobed leaves that were pale green above and whitish below. It was, Mark knew, a silver maple. According to Sparlow, there was only one such tree along that stretch of the stream. So he had reached the rendezvous at which he was to wait until the gambler joined him and had arrived without discovering so much as a single trace of a deer.

Coming to a halt behind a clump of bushes near the silver maple, the big blonde peered through them. No matter how he tried, he could not shake off a premonition that all was far from being well.

Was he the victim of a practical joke?

Would he be left at the tree until he grew tired of waiting and had to return to town, where Sparlow had already gone?

Although hunters frequently played practical jokes on their friends, Sparlow had not struck Mark as possessing that kind of humor. Certainly he had appeared to be very serious while discussing Viridian and Silky.

Even as that thought came, Mark saw a movement among the trees across the stream. Looking toward it, he found that Gianna Profaci was approaching with a small bundle of clothes in her hand. She was clad in a multicolored blouse, black skirt, and was barefoot.

On the point of rising and calling a greeting, Mark restrained himself. The woman was looking at the silver maple, then darted a glance upstream, as if she was expecting to see something—or some*body*. Halting by the water's edge, she made another examination of the trees and its surroundings. Then she turned toward a nearby clump of bushes and spoke. Mark was too far away to hear the words, but he guessed that she had asked a question. Giving the bushes a close scrutiny, the big blonde located a dark-gray patch that was neither leaves nor branches. Unless he was mistaken, it was the shoulder of a jacket; but that was all he could see of the man who was wearing it.

Gianna's behavior drew the blond giant's attention from the bushes. Giving a gesture of annoyance, she scowled once more in his direction without seeing him. Then she looked back over her shoulder. Dropping the bundle, she removed her blouse and skirt; leaving her with only a sleeveless white bodice and frilly-edged, knee-length panties. Attired in that scanty fashion, she knelt and picked a shirt from among the clothing to thrust it into the water.

Turning his eyes from the woman, Mark noticed that Viridian was walking toward her. What was more, although the big blonde suspected that she knew the hide and tallow man was coming, she gave no sign of it. Instead she threw another eager, searching glance across the stream. Then, as if having only just become aware of Viridian's presence, she stood up and faced him.

"What the hell's going on?" Mark said with a breath. "She acted like she was expecting to see somebody over this side of the stream. Which there's only Sparlow and me over here."

Easing around cautiously so that he would not betray his presence, the big blond searched the slope without locating the gambler. So he swung his gaze back toward the couple across the stream. From them he glanced to the clump of bushes. The patch of gray had gone, but he felt sure the man was still crouching in concealment.

Suddenly Mark realized what was happening. It was a trap for Viridian!

Other thoughts rushed through the blond giant's head. Why had Gianna been so interested in the maple tree? Everything in her attitude had suggested that she was expecting somebody to be near it. And it was the rendezvous selected by Sparlow for the end of their hunt.

It was possible, Mark decided, that the trap had been laid for him, and Viridian had inadvertently made an appearance.

Then a further alternative came to the big blonde. What if they were both *supposed* to be the victims?

On drawing the latter conclusion, Mark began to deduce what was supposed to have happened. If all had gone according to plan, he would have seen and joined Gianna. Finding them together, with her so scantily attired—she would probably have been embracing him—would have aroused Viridian's jealousy. After what Sparlow had told him about Viridian and Silky, a youngster like Mark was pretending to be would have responded in a manner that was sure to end in gunplay. Whichever of them had survived would have been killed by the man in the bushes.

Wanting to put this theories to a test, Mark first scanned the rim. When he still failed to locate Sparlow, he stepped from behind his place of concealment. Viridian was reaching toward Gianna but let out a curse and stepped back hurriedly. Surprise, suspicion, and annoyance flickered across the hide and tallow man's face, to be replaced by alarm as the big blonde snapped the Winchester's butt to his shoulder.

"Hey, you in the bushes!" Mark called, lining the rifle so that Viridian could see that it was not pointed at him. "Come out with your hands empty."

"What—?" Viridian barked, swiveling around with his right hand crossing toward the butt of the Remington.

There was a rustling among the foliage, and raising his empty hands, Shem rose into view calling, "Don't shoot!"

Instantly Gianna gave a startled squawk, which Mark would have taken for genuine if he had not known she was aware of the man's presence. Bending, she snatched up her blouse and skirt, holding them before her with what might have passed as becoming modesty under different circumstances.

"That's only *one* of you!" Mark went on, noticing that the man was wearing a brown suit. "If the others don't show themselves *pronto,* I'll put so much lead in, they'll be staying permanently."

"Come on out, Dub!" Shem advised, realizing that he was standing exposed to the big blond's rifle.

"That's a whole heap better," Mark declared as Dub appeared and joined his companion. "But if your big *amigo's* still hidden, you'd best ask him to get unhidden. Or shall I smoke him out by dropping you pair?"

"He ain't with us!" Dub stated, showing so much alarm that Mark believed him. "Is he, Dub?"

"That's the living truth, mister!" Dub affirmed, equally sure that the big blond would not hesitate to carry out the threat. He stared beyond Mark and raised his voice. "Silky ain't with us. Is he, Mr. Sparlow?"

"He'd better not be!" the gambler's voice roared from the slope beyond Mark's position. "And you shouldn't be either. Get the hell back to the New Orleans and I'll deal with you when I come."

Swinging his torso around, with the Winchester still held ready for use, Mark could not see Sparlow. Then the gambler came into view, carrying the Henry one-handed and striding down the slope. Slowly the big blond lowered his rifle, but he did not move.

For a moment Mark wondered why Sparlow had not tried to kill him. Then he knew the answer. Due to the suspicions that he had formulated with respect to the lack of deers' sign, he had instinctively made use of every bit of cover and avoided exposing himself any more than had been absolutely necessary. Just as he had been unable to see the gambler, Sparlow had failed to locate him.

Returning his gaze to the people beside the stream, Mark found that Gianna was dressing quickly. Watched by a scowling Viridian, Shem and Dub were hurrying away. Then Mark became aware of another person approaching. Dressed in a dark two-piece traveling costume, which she had not been wearing at breakfast, Marlene was walking toward her husband and carried a shotgun under her right arm.

Going to meet the gambler, Mark wondered if he could offer any explanation for what had been happening.

14

DID HE GET YOU, MARK?

Pivoting smoothly, the moment that the long-horned steer came to a halt at the end of the ramp's level section, Austin Viridian brought the poleax from where it had been resting on his shoulder. Despite his bulk and thickening waistline, he moved with speed and almost gracefully. Whistling through the air, the deadly implement swung at exactly the right height and parallel to the floor. The poleax had been made to his own specifications. At the end of its four-foot-six-inch-long handle, the head consisted of what looked like half a sledgehammer backed by a four-inch-long steel spike. The last two inches of the spike had been hollowed out in the fashion of a leather punch and for a similar purpose.

There was an almost exultant expression on the burly man's face as the spike of the poleax rushed toward its objective. On the point reaching the center of the steer's forehead, just below the boss of the horns, he let out a snort of elation. Before the animal had any chance of avoiding the attack, the point was slicing through the frontal bone of its skull. The weight of the hammerlike head gave an added impetus to the blow. With the sliver of bone that had been punctured out passing along the groove, the spike sank deeper until it reached the brain.

Killed instantly, the steer's forelegs started to buckle beneath it. As it collapsed, the Negro who was sharing the platform with Viridian pulled the lever in the wall. The level section of the ramp hinged downward, like the trap of a gallows opening. Pitched forward, the lifeless animal went sliding to the floor of the factory. Breathing heavily, Viridian turned and gazed after it.

Watched by Mark Counter, Gus Roxterby moved forward as the longhorn came to a halt. In his hands the supervisor was grasping a sharp-pointed and blood-smeared stick about a yard long. This was known as a pith-cane and performed an essential function in the slaughtering. Inserting the point into a neat hole caused by the poleax's steel spike, he pushed it onward until he located and destroyed the nerves of the spinal column. If that was not done, the nervous system could create reflex actions that—even after death—made the limbs kick unexpectedly and in a dangerous manner.

Until the two Negroes on the platform at the other side of the exit from the ramp that led to the holding corral hauled the level section back to horizontal, Viridian continued to scowl down at the blond giant. Thinking of what he had seen and heard since Mark's arrival, he decided that his wife had obtained a mighty dangerous and efficient ally. If it had not been for the big blonde, she would be dead. The sooner he was out of the way, the safer Viridian would feel.

Once the ramp hid the big youngster from view, Viridian swept his gaze around the vast room that formed the main portion of the factory. Maybe Marlene, Schweitzer, and the other two had had the finance, but it had been his knowledge that had made the factory the most efficient of its kind in Texas. Under his expert guidance, all the fixtures and fittings—including having the majority of the roof made from sheets of glass so that the work could continue even in inclement weather without the need for artificial lighting—had been laid out to facilitate the entire operation from holding the cattle to killing them and disposing of the unwanted portions of the carcasses.

From his point of vantage, Viridian could see practically the whole of the room. Behind him on the platform a lever in the wall controlled the ramp's trapdoor. It was returned to its level position by the two Negroes on the second platform. That was only the start of the operation.

Gazing down, Viridian satisfied himself that everything was progressing as it should be. Already the animals which had been slaughtered that day were being attended to by Roxterby and his Negro assistants. Having had the last-but-one-animal-to-die dragged to the skinning beds and turned onto its back, a colored man was starting to make the incision along its belly that was the prelude to stripping off the hide. Beyond him, working with deft speed, other Negroes were removing, flesh-ing, or otherwise preparing the skins of the earlier victims. A second party worked to separate the tallow—the harder, coarser fats of the body, which was used for among other things, making candles—from the skinned carcasses. When that task had been completed, the remains—including all of the meat, except the small amount appropriated by the Negroes— were pitched onto a wooden chute to slide into the Brazos River as it flowed through the Pilar Gorge.

Turning his eyes to the chute, Viridian could visualize what was happening at its lower end. He had often watched with amusement as the blue and flathead catfish swarmed to gorge upon the bloody flesh that was tumbling into the water.

Since the founding of the factory—and others of its kind— before the War Between the States, the Brazos River's popula-tion of blue *(Ictalurus Furcatus)* and flathead *(Pylodicitis Olivaris)* catfish had received so much food that they had multi-plied in numbers and grown to tremendous sizes. Viridian had seen many of both species in the gorge that exceeded fifty pounds in weight. There were even some that were up to three times that size. What was more, they had forsaken their normal nocturnal scavenging along the bottom and now rose high in the water to feed.

Although sufficient meat to have fed several families was disappearing down the disposal chute as he watched, Viridian felt no shame at such wanton waste. To his way of thinking, only the hides and tallow had any commercial value. The prices the company had been paying for the cattle were so low that the loss of the meat did not affect their profits.

Considering the latter point caused Viridian to think of his plans for the future. Before he could remove Marlene, he would have to get rid of the big blonde. Fortunately he had already worked out a way to do just that. All he needed was the right opportunity, and he knew that it would soon be granted to him.

"Hey, boss!" Leathers's voice came up the ramp from the corral. "Watch the next one, it's that big, mean old bastard of a bull."

"All right," Viridian answered. "I'll tell you when I want him."

"Yo!" Leathers replied. "He's in the chute and waiting."

Stepping to the edge of the platform, Viridian looked down. Adopting an amiable voice, he said, "What do you reckon about the way we do things, Mark?"

"I've never seen the beat of it," the blond giant admitted truthfully. Although he had visited a similar establishment at Brazoria, he knew that the Pilar Hide & Tallow Company's factory was far more efficient. "You can knock 'em down and skin 'em quicker than a hungry hound dog eating a stolen pie."

"How'd you like to try your hand at it?" Viridian inquired.

"Killing them?" Mark asked, then went on as the kind of youngster he was pretending to be would. "I'd like that fine."

"You don't start by killing them," Viridian warned, hoping that the big blonde was not familiar with the training of slaughtermen. "First off, you have to learn how to handle the pith-cane."

"All right, I'll give it a whirl," Mark promised, knowing that —in view of the interest he had expressed in the way the factory's work was carried out—to refuse might make Viridian suspicious. "Send one down and I'll do the sticking."

Even as Mark spoke, he wondered what was behind the offer.

While Viridian had brought him to the factory and had shown him around with obvious pride, the events of the morning had not been such that they led him to trust anybody connected with the Pilar Hide & Tallow Company.

Taken all in all, the blonde giant had never heard so much lying at one time as had taken place on the bank of the small stream. According to Sparlow, Dub and Shem had probably been doing nothing more than spying on the scantily attired Gianna. It was, he had pointed out, common knowledge that she invariably did her laundry in a similar state of undress. When Viridian had reminded him that she had previously only spent Monday morning at the task, Gianna had suggested that the pair could have heard her discussing the change of days with one of the women at the dance. Asked what had brought her into the woods, Marlene had replied that she had wanted a change from beef and so was hoping that she could shoot some rabbits. On his wife inquiring why he was there, Viridian had explained that he had come in the hope of finding Mark so as to invite him to spend the rest of the day at the factory.

Trying to sort out the facts from the fiction had left Mark more puzzled than enlightened.

On joining Mark, Sparlow had appeared to be subjecting his face to a careful scrutiny. Then, either because he was satisfied that the big blonde had suspected nothing or due to his being unaware of the trap, he had repeated his request that Mark not pick a fight with Viridian. Having crossed the stream, the gambler had apologized for the behavior of his men and had promised to deal with them on his return to the saloon. He had sounded so sincere that Mark had wondered if he might have been innocent. It was possible, the youngster had realized, that somebody else—Schweitzer had seemed a likely prospect—had conspired with Gianna and the two saloon workers.

With regard to the Italian woman, Mark had been just as confused. While Shem and Dub could have learned at the ball that she would be doing her laundry in the morning, most of her behavior had gone unexplained. Not only had she known the pair were watching, but she had been aware that Viridian was coming and had apparently expected to see somebody on the other side of the stream. While Mark had considered raising the puzzling points, he had decided against doing so at that time. By concealing the extent of his knowledge, he had hoped to learn if anybody else was sharing his suspicions.

The hope had not materialized.

Viridian's explanation for his presence might have been weak, but nobody had attempted to disprove it.

Going by the lack of comment Marlene's statement had aroused, Mark had concluded that it was not the first time she had hunted for rabbits. So although she had not mentioned a desire to change the menu at breakfast, she might have been speaking the truth. Of course, she might have been hoping to meet and talk privately with Mark, but that was unlikely. She would have known Sparlow would be nearby, if not with him. The only alternative Mark could envisage was that she had heard Gianna speak of going to the stream that morning and was hoping to catch her and Viridian in a compromising position.

Anyway, Mark told himself, he could hardly claim to have been a model of truthfulness. Instead of mentioning anything of what he had seen and suspected, he had pretended that he had noticed the two men skulking in the bushes while making for the maple but had not been able to see what they were watching. As soon as he had become aware that they were spying on Gianna, he had issued his challenge. Nothing in his story had suggested that he had been keeping the others under observation for at least a minute before announcing his presence.

Apparently everybody had been satisfied with each other's explanations. Certainly there had been no embarrassing questions asked. Even the matter of how Sparlow intended to deal with his employees had not been mentioned. Instead Marlene had suggested that they should all go to her house for coffee. If the speed with which the invitation was accepted had meant anything, there had been a mutual—if unspoken—disinclination to hold any further discussion on the incident. So they had chatted about inconsequential matters while drinking the coffee and then had gone their separate ways.

Even after leaving Sparlow outside the saloon, Viridian had not referred to the affair. Instead he had asked if Mark would consider taking control of branding the cattle that Ribagorza had delivered. While completing the remainder of their short journey, they had discussed how much the big blonde would be paid.

On their arrival Viridian had kept Mark occupied for a time with an inspection of the factory and by describing how it was operated. Then, having told him to look around and decide what he would require, Viridian had left him and gone into the main building. After completing his examination and having made his plans, Mark had followed. Viridian had been with Roxterby as he had entered, but had climbed up onto the killing platform before he had reached them. As there had not been room for the youngster to join his host, he had watched the work in progress. By noon he was growing bored and was not averse to being asked to participate.

Accepting the pith-cane from Roxterby, Mark glanced upward. He saw Viridian nod, then give a cheerful wave and turned away.

"Send him up!" Viridian called through the exit.

"Yo!" Leathers's voice responded, muffled by the gate at the lower end of the boxlike structure.

There was a creaking sound as the gate was raised, followed by a drumming of hooves as the bull passed through and a thud as it was lowered again. Silence fell as the bull, finding itself in the gloomy, inclined ramp, came to an uncertain halt. Then, seeing daylight ahead, it began to ascend. Wafting upward and into the ramp, the smell of blood that had been spilled by its predecessors reached the bull's nostrils. A low, deep, and awesome-sounding bellow echoed hollowly through the air.

"That's a bull, for sure," Mark commented to the floor supervisor. "Just listen to him give the blood call. No cow nor steer sounds that deep and mournful."

"Don't worry about it," Roxterby answered, moving to one side. "With the boss doing the killing, nothing can go wrong."

"I shouldn't think it would," Mark replied. "He drops them as dead as a six-day gone, stunk-up skunk."

Drawn onward by a combined wish to leave the passage and a desire to investigate the smell of the freshly spilled blood, which invariably exercised an irresistible fascination for its kind, the bull approached the top of the ramp. Big, powerful, with an enormous spread of needle-pointed horns, it was a magnificent example of the creatures that were destined to rebuild the state of Texas from hide and horn. It would have been capable of several more years of reproduction, passing on its excellent physical qualities to the advantage of the breed. Instead it was doomed to be slaughtered and disposed of in a very wasteful fashion.

Advancing in the confident manner of an animal that was sufficiently large and dangerous to have few natural enemies the bull started to pass through the exit. At the top of the ramp the floor became level for slightly more than the animal's length and was terminated just beyond the opening. Finding itself upon what must have seemed like the top of a cliff, the bull stopped. Its head and shoulders were exposed so that the slaughterman could do his work.

Giving the animal no time to realize the danger and retreat, Viridian swung the poleax. He seemed to be striking as he had on the previous occasions, but there was one very important difference. After he had spoken to Mark, he had changed the way in which he was grasping the handle.

The hammerlike section made the contact instead of the spike!

Although the bull crumpled forward, it was only stunned. Unaware of what had happened and seeing the animal collapsing in what appeared to be the usual manner, the Negro threw the trapdoor's lever. The dazed, but far from incapacitated, longhorn was precipitated on to the floor below.

Grasping the pith-cane ready for use, Mark walked forward to carry out his task. He had watched the other victims of the poleax sliding lifeless down the ramp and saw nothing different in the way that the bull arrived.

"Hey, Mr. Counter!" Roxterby called.

"Yes?" Mark inquired, looking over his shoulder but continuing to approach the animal.

"Whatever you do," the supervisor began, "make sure that—"

"Watch out, mister!" yelled one of the Negroes who were moving forward ready to drag the carcass to the skinning beds. "It's not dead!"

The last sentence of the warning was drowned out by an explosive, rage-filled snort from just ahead of the blond giant. Not that he needed to hear the words to know what had caused them. He had heard enraged long-horned bulls often enough to be able to identify the sound for what it was.

Swinging his gaze to the front, the big blonde found exactly what he had expected to see—that he was in serious danger.

Not that Mark was given an opportunity to consider the matter at length. Unlike more domesticated breeds of cattle, a Texas longhorn did not lurch up rump-first, pausing on its knees to "pray," as the cowhands called the action. Instead it bounded to its feet with surprising speed for so large a creature. All in what appeared to be one continuous flow of motion, it rose, lunged forward, lowered, then whipped up its head in a swing that directed its horns at the nearest living object—the big Texan.

Never had Mark better cause to be grateful for his quick wits and lightning-fast reactions. Watching the bull's head rising toward him, he observed that the tip of the left horn was ingrained with dirt. That implied it was what he had heard Mexican *vaqueros*—with their knowledge gained from bullfighters—describe as the "master horn," the one favored by the animal when launching an attack. He noticed something else about the animal's head, but in the urgency of the situation his mind failed to register what it might be. Before he could decide, he was flinging himself backward and to his left.

There was the crash of a shot from behind and to the right of

Mark. He felt something tug sharply at the inside of his right
sleeve. Then he realized that the bullet must have cut through
the material, without touching his flesh, in passing. Not that he
gave the matter much thought. There were other things to oc-
cupy his attention. The horn could not have missed him by
more than three inches. However, his rearward bound carried
him clear, and the bull was going by. He landed with his right
hand diving to the butt of its Colt, for he knew that the enraged
and wounded creature—the lead had ended its flight in the
bull's chest—would have to be killed before it attacked another
person.

Twice more Roxterby's short-barreled weapon roared as he
retreated rapidly before the approaching bull. Behind him, the
colored men scattered as fast as their legs would carry them.
None of them was armed, and they all knew just how dangerous the charging animal could be. Both bullets followed the
first into its chest cavity. The shots merged in with the rolling
thunder of Mark's Colt.

Catching his balance on alighting, the big blonde completed
his draw. He pressed his right elbow tight against his ribs, held
back the trigger, and used the heel of his left hand to manipu-
late the hammer. Fanning was not a means to be employed if
extreme accuracy was required, but—when performed by an
expert such as Mark—there was no faster way of throwing lead
from a single-action revolver. What was more, he was directing
the bullets at a large target. Pivoting his whole body, rather
than turning the barrel, he sent shot after shot into the animal's
shoulder, barrel, loin, and rump.

Reeling, the stricken bull went down. Almost as soon as it
had fallen, Sparlow sprang forward. He thrust his revolver's
muzzle against the point where the spike of the poleax should
have landed and squeezed the trigger. There was a spasmodic
heave, and then the mighty body went limp.

"What the hell happened?" Viridian demanded, having
sprung to the edge of the platform as if attracted by the commotion. He hoped that his disappointment did not show as he

looked at the blond giant and went on, "Did he get you, Mark?"

"Nope," the big blonde answered. "But it was mighty close."

Poleax in hand, Viridian hurried down the steps from the platform. Returning his revolver to its holster, Roxterby watched as Mark walked toward him. However, the big blonde put away his Colt and bent to look at the hole in the bull's head. Darting a glance at Viridian, the supervisor received a scowl in return. However, he had more to worry about than having failed to carry out the hide and tallow man's instructions.

"I thought I was going to hit you," Roxterby said as Mark straightened up and looked at him. The explanation was, in part, also designed to exculpate him with his employer. "You jumped between me and the bull just as I was pulling the trigger."

"It seemed like a good thing to be doing at the time," Mark answered, wondering if there had not been a wound in the bull's head as it rose to attack him. "Anyway, there's no real harm done, except for a nick in my sleeve. And I'd rather it was there than in me." He turned to Viridian, continuing, "What the hell went wrong, Austin?"

"It must have started to drop its head just as I hit," the burly man replied. "So it was only stunned. I've had it happen before, haven't I, Mr. Roxterby."

"More than once, boss," the supervisor agreed, silently cursing his bad luck. "That's why I was ready to start shooting."

Although Viridian had refused to part with more than two hundred and fifty dollars, due to Widge's failure to kill Marlene as well as de Froissart, he had offered to make up the full amount if Roxterby would perform another service. The supervisor was supposed to shoot the big blonde if the bull failed to gore him.

Knowing that there was no way he could prove otherwise, Mark accepted the explanation. However, he had no intention of placing himself in a similar situation. So he stated that he would leave the slaughtering and use of the pith-cane to experts.

"Being a cowhand's good enough for me," Mark finished. "And I reckon I'll do something I know I can handle. So I'll go and see about that branding you want doing."

"Just sing out if there's anything you need," Viridian offered, satisfied that the youngster did not suspect the truth about the "accident."

"I'll want three or four OD Connected branding irons made up," Mark requested.

"Why?" Viridian inquired.

"To make the brands look natural," Mark explained. "I don't reckon any of you men can handle a running iron well enough to do that. And those ranchers who're coming have enough cow-savvy to know the difference."

There was another point, although Mark had no intention of mentioning it. The copies of the OD Connected's branding iron would be evidence to disprove the lies that the partners were planning to tell Ole Devil Hardin.

"How do we get them?" Viridian asked.

"I'll have the blacksmith make them up," Mark replied. "It's not a hard job."

"I'll come with you so that he won't ask any questions," Viridian declared, wanting to prevent the youngster from being with his wife when he was not present.

Although Mark guessed what was behind the suggestion, he did not argue. However, before they could leave, a herd of a hundred head was delivered. None of the men who accompanied it had been in Fort Worth, and they were eager to hear about the result of the Ranch Owners' Convention. While Viridian had been talking with their leader in the office, the rest of the men drove the cattle into the large corral, which already was holding Ribagorza's unbranded stock. Leathers did not know about the use to which the Mexican's cattle were to be put, and Mark refrained from enlightening him. On discovering what had happened, after the men had left to collect their money from Schweitzer, Viridian insisted that the two bunches be separated. Doing so took the rest of the afternoon.

An annoyed Viridian accompanied Mark to Pilar. He blamed Leathers for the extra work and inconvenience, due to the youngster having claimed that he was using the backhouse when the two herds had been allowed to mingle. They were riding by the jailhouse when Viridian heard his name called. Looking around, they saw Schweitzer coming from the building. From the expression on his face, something appeared to be disturbing him.

"Hi, Bernie," Viridian said in greeting, bringing his horse to a halt. Although puzzled by the look on his partner's face, he went on, "Did you pay those fellers—?"

"Austin!" the storekeeper interrupted, his face working with anxiety. "Austin. It's—It's—Joe!"

"Joe," Viridian repeated, dismounting. "You mean Joe Profaci?"

"Yes!" Schweitzer confirmed.

"What's wrong with him?" Viridian asked.

"This deputy's just arrived from Bryan," Schweitzer explained, jerking a thumb to where a leathery old-timer wearing a peace officer's badge was coming from the building followed by Jesse Sparlow. "He says they found Joe's body in a draw about five miles south of town. He'd been robbed and murdered."

"When did it happen?" Viridian demanded, without displaying any of the distress that his partner was exhibiting.

"Two, three days back, according to the doctor," the Bryan lawman replied. "He allows it must've happened around Sunday."

15
NOW I'LL *HAVE* TO KILL YOU

Marlene Viridian was in anything but a pleasant temper as she swept downstairs and glowered around the deserted entrance hall of her mansion. Clad in a diaphanous nightdress, over which she had drawn a negligee that was no more substantial, and with slippers on her bare feet, she had clearly not been long out of bed. The time was almost noon, but early rising had never been one of her virtues.

Despite Marlene's repeated tugs at the bell rope by her bed, her maid had not arrived with breakfast and to help her dress. Nor had her shouts from the door of the bedroom produced any response. So, donning her negligee, she had come to find out what was causing the delay. For all the signs of life, she might have had the big house to herself.

"Henry! Marge!" Marlene yelled, glaring about her furiously. "Where the hell are you? Come here, damn it!"

There was no reply. Scowling malevolently and promising to fire every one of the servants, Marlene stalked across the hall and looked into her husband's study. It was deserted and from there she went to the sitting room. Opening the door, she let out a low, puzzled exclamation. Dressed as she had been the previous morning and barefooted as she so frequently went, Gianna Profaci was sitting on the *chaise longue.*

"What the hell—?" Marlene began. "Who let you in?"

"That's not a nice way to talk to the grieving widow of your dead partner," the Italian woman complained, although little in her tone or appearance qualified her for such a description. She came to her feet, picking up the vanity bag that had been by her side. "But, then, you never have been polite to me, have you?"

"Have you seen the servants?" Marlene demanded, ignoring the comment and walking forward.

"Yes," Gianna replied, and slipped her right hand into the mouth of the bag. "I told them to go home—"

"You've done *what?*" Marlene yelped, her voice rising higher with each word.

"I've sent them home," Gianna answered, and a mocking smile played on her lips. "As we've always been such *good* friends, I didn't think you'd want them around to see me arrest you."

At about the same time that Gianna was making her remarkable statement to Marlene, Mark Counter was standing talking with Austin Viridian and Gus Roxterby by the factory's disposal chute. All around them, the bustle of working men went on.

The big blonde had seen little to suggest that the hide and tallow man had regretted the death of his second partner. Rather, Viridian had appeared puzzled and worried, but not nearly as much as Schweitzer had been. The storekeeper had seemed to be very alarmed and almost frightened by the news.

Acting in his capacity as constable, Jesse Sparlow had asked both partners to join him in the jailhouse's office to discuss the matter. Although Mark had not been included in the invitation, nobody had raised objections when he had gone with them.

According to the deputy who had brought the news from Bryan, the body had been found by two men who were out hunting. An examination of the tracks in the vicinity had suggested that Profaci had been killed elsewhere, then carried across his saddle and thrown into the draw. He had been shot in the back, probably with a rifle, and his pockets had been emptied. As yet, his horse had not been located.

Questioned by Sparlow, the deputy had said that there had been no footprints or anything else to supply a clue to the murderer's identity. However, it had appeared that only one man was involved. Without waiting to be asked, the gambler had given account of his movements while in Bryan. He had spent the evening and night in the company of a girl who worked in the Two Bulls Saloon, leaving her at around noon on Sunday and returning along the stagecoach trail to Pilar. The deputy had then claimed that Profaci had taken his departure, heading south, shortly after sunup. While that had not completely exonerated Sparlow, it had provided him with a reasonably sound alibi. If the two partners had been suspicious of him, they had concealed their feelings.

Studying Viridian and Schweitzer as the meeting had drawn to an inconclusive end, Mark guessed at their sentiments and what was causing their anxious attitudes. While they probably were pleased with the thought that there were now two less to share in the company's profits, they had been disturbed by the thought that Profaci might have been carrying his copy of the statement. They were already worried by the possibility of Harlow Dolman's copy falling into the wrong hands, for Mark had not enlightened them on the subject. Nor had there been any word of the Captain's body having been found, despite the partners' request that—as he was a good friend—they should be informed.

While guessing at the cause of the two men's perturbation, Mark had known that one of the statements was no longer a cause for alarm to them. The previous evening, during a brief absence of Viridian, Marlene had told Mark that she had had to confess to her husband and Schweitzer that she had destroyed de Froissart's copy.

The evening had passed uneventfully, although Viridian had been understandably restless. Neither he nor Marlene had been able to make any clear decision upon Profaci's murder, although she had commented on Gianna's lack of emotion to the news. On being told of her husband's death, the Italian woman had crossed herself and said something in her native tongue. Then she had turned her back on them and requested that they leave her to pray for him. At no time had she displayed any of the grief that might have been expected from a person of her volatile nature. Nor would she allow Marlene either to stay with her or to have one of the townswomen do so. Marlene had attributed her lack of emotion to the fact that she had never loved her frequently tyrannical husband and was most likely delighted to be rid of him.

Marlene had still been in bed when Mark had left for the factory with Viridian that morning. They had called at the blacksmith's shop and found that he had just made a start at producing the first of the fake OD Connected branding irons. Mark had wondered what reason the hide and tallow man had given when asking for them to be made, but was too wise to speak about it.

In passing, the big blonde and Viridian had noticed a sign reading CLOSED FOR INVENTORY in the general store's window. The burly man had commented that it was unusual for Schweitzer to take an inventory of his stock on a weekday, but did not pay a visit to his partner. The New Orleans had been closed, which was not surprising as it was never opened before noon.

Still wondering if Viridian's failure to kill the bull might have been intentional and not accidental, Mark had declined when it had been suggested that he should help with the slaughtering. Then he had made a counterproposal that had prevented his host from pressing the matter. With Viridian's approval, he and several Negroes had spent the morning examining the hides that were awaiting shipment. Every one they found to be without a brand had been put aside so that it could later be marked with the OD Connected and used in the deception. As Mark had every intention of spoiling the partners' plot, he had had no qualms about putting such an idea into Viridian's head.

Having completed the task, the big blonde had entered the

factory meaning to tell Viridian that he was going to the New Orleans Saloon for a meal and a drink. However, before he could do so, the hide and tallow man had asked if he had ever seen what happened to the meat that was thrown into the river. Although Mark had had an idea of what to expect, having watched the disposal process at the factory in Brazoria, he had refrained from mentioning the fact. Instead he had gone with Viridian and Roxterby to the chute.

"Just look at that big bastard!" Viridian exclaimed, pointing to where the back and deeply forked tail of a massive blue catfish bulged up through the churning, bloody surface in its eagerness to reach the gory carcass that had just tumbled into the water. "There's some even bigger than him."

"A man could have him a jim-dandy time fishing hereabouts," Mark answered. "But he'd likely have to use a dead cow for bait. Well, I reckon I'll be——."

"Hello," Roxterby put in, staring at the open double doors. "I wonder what they're wanting here?"

Turning his head, Mark saw that Sparlow was entering followed by Shem and Dub. The trio formed a rough arrowhead formation as they advanced across the room. To the big blonde's way of thinking, there was something significant and almost sinister in the manner in which they were approaching. The gambler was empty-handed, but he had thrust back the left side of his jacket to leave the butt of his revolver exposed. Each of his companions had a sawed-off shotgun dangling by the wrist of its butt in his right fist. While the barrels were pointing at the floor, they could easily be tilted into alignment. All in all, they had the appearance of men who were expecting trouble.

"Hello, Sparlow," Viridian said in greeting as the trio came to a halt about fifteen feet away. "What brings you here?"

"A couple of things," the gambler replied, flickering a glance at the killing platform. "I figured you'd want to know that I've found out who killed Hubric and set Twickery free."

"You're damned right I do!" Viridian declared. "Who was it?"

"Your partner," Sparlow answered.

"My *partner?*" the hide and tallow man spat out. "You mean it was Bernie Schweitzer?"

"That's just who it was."

"But how—?"

"He slipped out of his store at around eleven and sneaked over to the jailhouse without being seen. Of course Hubric didn't hesitate to let him in. He knifed him in the back when he turned to take him to see Twickery and sat him in the chair so's anybody who looked in'd think he was asleep. Then he made a deal with Twickery and sent him after you."

"The lousy son of a bitch!" Viridian said.

"Where—?"

"How'd you find it out, Jesse?" Mark inquired, cutting off the other's angry question.

"I'd an idea who it was from the start," Sparlow replied, and threw another look at the exit from the corral's chute. "I didn't let on, but I found close to five hundred dollars when I searched Twickery's body at the jail. And he'd lost all the money he'd got for his skins at the saloon before we had to put him to sleep."

"Where's Schweitzer now?" Viridian snarled.

"Gone," Sparlow told him, and once again turned a quick gaze at the killing platform. Then he made what Mark, watching him carefully, took to be a brief but impatient gesture before continuing, "I think he must have guessed that I was on to him, because he lit out early this morning."

"He got away?" the hide and tallow man almost bellowed.

"Well, no," the gambler answered, looking from Mark to Viridian, then at Roxterby, who was standing silently at his employer's left side. "We went after him as soon as we found he'd gone. Caught him on the trail, but he resisted arrest."

"He's dead, huh?" Mark drawled, noticing that Sparlow's companions also seemed to be dividing their attention between his party and the killing platform.

"Dead as they come," the gambler confirmed. "He tried to draw as we rode up. I tried to wound him, but his horse must have moved—"

"Nobody blames you for that," Viridian stated magnani-mously, being delighted to learn that he had only one partner left alive.

"*You* couldn't anyway," Sparlow replied, reaching under his coat toward his hip pocket with his right hand. "He'd've been dead already if Twickery hadn't met you on Monday night when you was going to burn him out with that can of ker-osene."

"I'm in no mood to listen to stupid jokes!" Marlene spat at the Italian woman.

"It's no joke," Gianna replied. "Jesse Sparlow's made me his deputy and said I was to arrest you as an access—access—because you're mixed up in Austin killing that rancher in Fort Worth."

Marlene sucked in a deep breath and stared at Gianna for a moment. Then, before she could stop herself, she asked, "Did Joe tell you about that?"

"*Him?*" Gianna snorted. "That fat son of a bitch never told me nothing."

"Then how did you know—?" Marlene began, her eyes going to the sidepiece as she remembered there was a loaded Reming-ton Double Derringer in its center drawer.

"Jesse found these papers—" Gianna began.

"On Joe's body?" Marlene interrupted, having heard about Profaci's murder and guessing that the gambler had killed him.

"No," Gianna replied, being so delighted by the situation that she could not resist explaining. By doing so, she inadver-tently confirmed her rival's suspicions. "Jesse said he must have had a copy, but he didn't have it on him."

"Then how could you know about it?" Marlene inquired, starting to move slowly in the direction of the sidepiece without turning or taking her eyes from the other woman.

"Jesse took three copies from Bernie Schweitzer this morn-ing. And a contract that the rancher had signed. He says that contract proves Austin killed the rancher."

"The stupid bastard!" Marlene raged. "We told him to get rid—You got it from *Bernie*?"

"Jesse did," Gianna corrected, deriving pleasure from the other woman's response to her news. Ever since they had first met, Marlene had made it plain that she did not regard her as a social equal. In fact the treatment she had received at the other woman's hands had been closer to that afforded to the servants. It was very satisfying to be the cause of so much perturbation and concern. "He said Bernie told him that he'd taken it from the safe at the factory after the dance."

"So the sly old bastard had a key!" Marlene breathed, then she glared at the Italian woman. "Are you serious about Sparlow sending you to arrest me?"

"I said I'd do it while he took the boys and killed Austin—" Gianna replied, bringing the words to a halt as if suddenly realizing that she had made a slip of the tongue. Such was her hatred of the other woman that she could not resist playing a cat-and-mouse game, so she gasped, "What I just said!" Then she shrugged her shoulders and started to withdraw her hand from the vanity bag and allowed it to fall as she did so. "I've said too much. Now I'll *have* to kill you. I told Jesse that I mi—"

The hand held a spear-pointed knife.

When thinking about how she would deal with the situation, Gianna had tried to guess what Marlene's reaction would be to the sight of the knife. A scream of terror followed by fainting, an attempt to run away, or to be begged for mercy had all crossed her mind. However, the response she received was far different from anything she had envisaged.

At the sight of the dangerous-looking weapon, Marlene did not hesitate. As Gianna advanced, confident that the other woman would do one of the things that she had considered, she ran into a roundhouse slap. Marlene's right palm struck her left cheek with a resounding crack. Taken unawares by the speed and force of the attack, Gianna was knocked staggering for a few paces and lost her hold on the knife.

Turning as soon as she had delivered the blow. Marlene

darted toward the sidepiece. Just as she was jerking open the drawer, she heard the patter of rapidly approaching footsteps. Before their meaning struck her, fingers were grasping the neck of the negligee from behind and another hand grabbed her by the shoulder.

Guessing what Marlene had in mind, Gianna paid no attention to the pain caused by the slap or the tears it had brought to her eyes. Dashing forward, she grabbed hold of the first things her fingers touched and, pivoting, she heaved the other woman away from the drawer. Yelling in alarm, Marlene felt her arms slip from the negligee's sleeves. She left the garment in her assailant's hands as she was propelled across the room.

Stumbling against the table, Marlene was brought to a halt. Twisting around, she saw Gianna rushing at her with hands extended and crooked like the talons of a bird of prey. Her antipathy toward the Italian woman combined with rage and not a little fear to make her respond in a similar manner. Out shot her own arms, driving fingers into hair as she thrust herself forward to meet her attacker. Even as she felt as if her scalp was being ripped off, she began to tear at the fists full of black locks.

Uttering gasps, squeals, and what they might have imagined were words but emerged as almost animallike croaks, the two women clung to hair and circled with legs flailing in wild kicks. Still entangled, they fell onto and rolled across the table to tumble side by side to the floor. Still they did not part. Maintaining one hand in the other woman's hair, each of them used the second to slap, punch, claw, and grab constantly as they turned and thrashed over and over along the floor. All of their mutually pent-up hatred was being unleased, causing them to ignore the punishment they were receiving in their eagerness to inflict pain and suffering upon the other woman.

At last, gasping in exhaustion, they rolled apart. Three continuous minutes of mindless brawling had left Marlene naked and Gianna bare to the waist. Their hair was in matted tangles, sweat soaked them, while blood flowed from their nostrils, lips, and flesh, bitten when the opportunity had arisen.

For a few seconds the two women lay supine, bosoms heaving as they sought to replenish their lungs with air. Then as if on a signal, they rolled onto their hands and knees. Gianna made the next move. Every inch of her gorgeous body throbbed with a variety of aches. Sobbing for breath, she gazed through tear-blurred eyes until she located the knife. Then she dived forward, with her hands shooting ahead. Before she could grasp the hilt, she felt Marlene catch hold of her skirt's hem. Wriggling onward, while her attacker tried to drag her back, she was conscious of the garment losing its hold on her waist. Giving a sudden writhe, she drew herself free. A moment later she had the hilt of the knife in her hand.

Realization of her peril lent speed to Marlene's movements. Throwing aside the skirt, she rolled desperately to put some distance between herself and Gianna. Then she started to rise. The Italian woman was also getting up. Once on their feet, they rushed at each other without any thought of the possible consequences. More by luck than by intent, Marlene managed to catch hold of Gianna's right wrist in both her hands. Instinct guided the response made by Gianna. Bringing her knee upward between Marlene's spread-apart thighs, she jabbed it into her vulva region. While the attack was not delivered with exceptional force, it was severe enough to cause Marlene to lose her grip on the wrist. From it, her hands went to press against Gianna's bare, heaving bosom. Bringing the knife around and up, Gianna sank its point into Marlene's belly and ripped sideways. Agony sent a spasm through the stricken woman. Screaming, she thrust Gianna away from her with a violent shove. Although hurled backward, the Italian woman contrived to retain her grasp on the knife and it was snatched free from Marlene's flesh.

With blood pouring from the wound, Marlene turned and stumbled against the sidepiece. Remembrance of what the open drawer held came to her. Dipping her hand in, she picked up the Remington Double Derringer. Enfolding the bird's-head butt in both fists, she swung around to confront Gianna. Rushing forward, the Italian woman saw the gun pointing in her

direction. Before the complete understanding of what it meant
sank in, Marlene had drawn back the hammer and squeezed
the trigger. They were so close together that she could not miss.
Flying upward, the .41-caliber bullet punctured Gianna's cheek
just beneath the left eye and continued its passage into her
brain. She fell forward with the knife slipping out of her hand,
to collapse against Marlene. They went to the floor together.
Slowly, painfully, Marlene rolled the lifeless woman from her
and began to crawl across the room. She knew that she was
hurt badly, but did not realize that she was bleeding to death.
Even if there had been trained help available, it was unlikely
that she could have been saved. As it was, she was alone in the
mansion.

"You're making a damned bad mistake, Sparlow," Viridian
warned. "Twickery was bringing the kerosene—."

"You were going to come into town wearing a sombrero and
poncho—" the gambler corrected, but was not allowed to continue.

"How did you know?" Viridian demanded. "I fetched them
in the next morning and nobody'd seen me wear—*Gianna*! The
lousy little bitch told you!"

"You're talking about the woman I'm going to marry,"
Sparlow interrupted, throwing yet another quick look at the
killing platform. He did not offer to take his right hand from
the hip pocket as he went on. "Every time I went to see her,
damned if she didn't have something new to tell me. If it's any
interest to you, Bernie had double-crossed you. He'd got a
spare key to the safe in your office—"

"God damn it to hell!" Viridian bellowed, realizing what
could have happened. "If he'd opened it—"

"He did," Sparlow declared. "Those statements make interesting reading, taken with the contract Paul Dover signed. Its
date shows he must have signed it the day he was murdered."

Although Mark had been listening to the conversation and
knew that he had finally obtained proof of Viridian's guilt, he
wondered whether he would be allowed to make use of his

knowledge. Clearly Sparlow intended to use Gianna as a means of gaining control of the Pilar Hide & Tallow Company. Which implied that, like Schweitzer, Viridian was to be killed "resisting arrest." Even if the gambler did not suspect that Marlene hoped to use Mark to back up her bid for domination of the company, he would not be likely to leave witnesses to testify to what had really happened. The Negroes were overtly watching what went on, but Sparlow would know that their testimony would not be called for if the state police conducted an inquiry. The investigating officers would not want to antagonize such a potentially influential man as Sparlow would be after the deaths of all the original partners. However, Mark and, to a lesser extent, Roxterby were a different matter. They could not be overlooked if they were still alive.

Thinking about the latter point, Mark was also puzzled by the interest Sparlow and his companions had kept showing in the killing platform. No cattle had been sent up it for some time—

Even as Mark considered the latter aspect and guessed what was happening, he saw a big shape appearing at the exit from the ramp. It was Silky, and he held a Henry rifle.

Then most of the points that had puzzled the blond giant became clear.

Sparlow and his two companions had been too far away to chance opening fire as soon as they had entered the building. So they had moved to a range over which their weapons would be satisfactory. In addition they had also taken the precaution of having unsuspected support from another position. However, for some reason Silky had been delayed.* So Sparlow had been compelled to keep Viridian's party occupied in conversation.

---

* Mark learned later that Leathers had been in the backhouse when Silky had gone to deal with him and effect an entrance via the ramp. Then, having clubbed the supervisor unconscious with the butt of the rifle he had been loaned by Sparlow, Silky had had to wait until the Negro corral hands had driven a longhorn back out of the chute and opened the gate so he could make his belated ascent to the factory.

"Get 'em, b——!" Silky bellowed, halting at the end of the ramp and starting to lift the rifle's butt toward his shoulder.

That was as far as the burly saloon worker got with his advice. Seeing him appear, the Negro who was in charge of the lever pulled it. Silky's third word changed into a startled yell as the floor collapsed beneath his feet. Loosing his grasp on the Henry, he plunged downward.

Having observed their companion's arrival, Sparlow, Shem, and Dub were ready to go into action. While puzzled by Silky's delayed appearance, the gambler had to admit that it was well timed. Rage was contorting Viridian's face and, before the comment about Dover's contract had ended, his right hand was flying across to the butt of the Remington. An instant after his boss had started to draw, Roxterby was grabbing with considerable speed toward his Colt. So was the big blonde.

Even as Sparlow's mind was noting the details, he, too, was making his draw. Not with the right hand, however. He had placed that in his hip pocket to lull his victims into a sense of false security. Turning palm out, his left hand snapped to the forward-pointing butt of his Colt and snapped it from its holster. On either side of him, Shem and Dub pivoted the barrels of their shotguns upward, and their empty hands reached for the foregrips.

Although Viridian and Roxterby had made their moves just that vital split second ahead of the others, they were distracted by the commotion as the trapdoor was dropped from under Silky. First to clear leather, due to the advantage he gained by having reduced the length of his revolver's barrel, the supervisor was on the point of shooting at Dub. Instead he hesitated due to his eyes turning toward the ramp. There was a double roar from Dub's shotgun, for he did not intend to take the chance of Roxterby recovering and throwing lead at him. Eighteen buckshot balls arrived with enough force to fling the supervisor backward into the wall, whence he bounced lifeless to the floor.

To Sparlow's horror, he found that Viridian was much faster than he had imagined. Before his own weapon had left its holster, he saw the Remington turning toward him and knew there was no way in which he might stop it being fired.

Fate took a hand and gave the gambler a respite.

Unlike his companions, Mark had been aware of Silky's presence. With his hands leaping toward the ivory handles of the matched Colts, he had kept his eyes on the saloon worker. Seeing what the Negro was doing, the blond giant snapped his gaze to the more immediate threat to his life—and not a moment too soon. Shem was turning the twin tubes of the shotgun upward in his direction. However, without the need for conscious guidance, the revolvers had left their contoured holsters and were lining instinctively. Without trying to establish his exact point of aim, he squeezed a shot from the right-hand weapon.

When the lead plowed into his left breast, Shem was twisted around. Although he jerked at the forward trigger, the shotgun was no longer pointing at Mark. Instead the balls rushed out and almost tore Viridian's right arm from his shoulder. Twirling helplessly, the Remington toppling out of a hand that had suddenly become inoperative, he hit the end of the disposal chute and fell forward. The planks were wet and slippery with blood, so he started to slide down them.

Unable to change his aim, or even to avoid firing, Sparlow sent his bullet off just after the buckshot had found its unintended target. Then, as the hide and tallow man disappeared, the gambler thumbed back his Colt's hammer and started to turn it on the blond giant.

Thinking and acting with lightning speed, Mark saw that he was in double danger. Not only was Sparlow trying to throw down on him, but Dub had flung aside what must be an empty weapon and was clawing for his holstered revolver. Mark did not have time to check on what had happened to Roxterby, but he felt sure that Dub had not missed the supervisor over such a short distance. In which case the saloon worker would be after him next.

Pointing his left-hand Colt under his right arm as it rose with the other revolver's recoil, the blond giant squeezed its trigger.

Flame rushed from the muzzle and a hole appeared just above Sparlow's right eye. His head snapped to the rear and he went down with his weapon unfired.

That left Dub. Twisting his torso, Mark started to turn lead loose. Right, left, right, left and right again, the weapons roared consecutively and at such speed that the detonations formed into a volley as fast as he could have achieved when handling his Winchester. Powder smoke rolled, partially concealing him and obscuring his target. Luck stayed with Mark. Only one of the bullets found flesh, but it served its purpose by shattering Dub's right arm. The man's revolver bellowed, but it had been deflected just enough. Mark felt the wind of the bullet against his cheek as it flew by.

Slowly the smoke swirled away and, now that the guns had stopped roaring, Mark became conscious of the Negroes' voices being raised in excited conversation on all sides. Cocking his right-hand revolver, the big blonde looked about him. Sparlow was dead. From the look of them, Shem and Dub were too badly injured to continue the fight. One glance informed Mark that the same applied to Silky. Having landed awkwardly, he was writhing on the floor and holding what proved to be a leg with a compound fracture.

Satisfied that none of his enemies was in any condition to cause further mischief, Mark sprang to the disposal chute. Staring down, he saw Viridian. Despite the hideous wound, the man was still alive. However, he was pouring blood into the water. Even as Mark looked, a huge body flashed from the depths. Two more followed, converging on Viridian. He screamed once and briefly as the monsters he had helped to create closed their jaws on his limbs. The sound was chopped off abruptly as he was dragged below the surface and more of the catfish rushed in to rend at his flesh.

A shudder ran through the big youngster and he turned away. Returning the smoking Colts to their holsters, he called to some of the Negroes to attend to the wounded men. Then he walked slowly toward the factory's entrance. He would have to go into Pilar and tell the citizens what had happened.* Then he would have to make arrangements for Marlene and Gianna to be held in custody. He wondered what their fate would be. One thing he felt was sure, both were so involved in the various murderous plots of the hide and tallow men that it was unlikely that they would be able to carry on operating the factory.

Not until Mark reached the Viridians' mansion did he discover just how true that assumption had been.

---

* There were a few points that Mark was unable to clear up, as he never learned the answers:

Schweitzer and Profaci had plotted to remove their other partners when they had learned that Goodnight's scheme was gaining acceptance. The Italian had been on his way to Houston, to hire men to carry out the removals. Meeting Gomez in Bryan and learning of the trouble with Ribagorza, Profaci had paid the Mexican to visit the factory and use the demand for advance payment as an excuse to kill Viridian.

Learning from Gianna of her husband's departure, Sparlow had set off after him and murdered him, hiding his body and leaving his horse tied up in the woods. The dance-hall girl admitted that she had been paid to supply him with an alibi.

Schweitzer's decision to leave Pilar had come when he had heard of Profaci's death. Already suspicious of Viridian, guessing that he had been responsible for de Froissart's murder and the truth about the can of kerosene, he had also believed that Sparlow was hoping to gain control of the company. So, having taken the precaution of obtaining a spare key for the safe at the factory's office, he had collected Viridian's copies of the statement and the incriminating contract. Knowing that he would be able to call upon men hired by Profaci, he had taken the documents and all his money, then had set off with the intention of returning when he had sufficient helpers to protect his interests. On discovering that the storekeeper had fled, Sparlow had given chase. In the hope of saving his life, Schweitzer had handed over the documents and explained how they could be used. The hope had not materialized. Sparlow had killed him and had set out to complete the task by getting rid of the Viridians. Being short of men, he had yielded to Gianna's request to be allowed to deal with Marlene.

APPENDIX 1

During the War Between the States at seventeen years of age, Dustine Edward Marsden Fog had won promotion in the field and was put in command of the Texas Light Cavalry's hard-riding, harder-fighting Company C. Leading them in the Arkansas Campaign, he had earned the reputation for being an exceptionally capable military raider the equal of the South's other exponents, John Singleton Mosby and Turner Ashby. In addition to preventing a pair of Union fanatics from starting an Indian uprising, which would have decimated most of Texas, he had supported Belle Boyd, the Rebel spy, on two of her most dangerous missions.

When the war had finished, he had become the segundo *of the great OD Connected Ranch in Rio Hondo County, Texas. Its owner and his uncle, General Ole Devil Hardin, had been crippled in a riding accident, and it had thrown much of the work—including handling an important mission upon which the good relations between the United States and Mexico had hung in the balance—upon him. After helping to gather horses to replenish the ranch's depleted remuda, he had been sent to assist Colonel Charles Goodnight on the trail drive to Fort Sumner, which had done much to help the Lone Star State to recover from the impoverished conditions left by the war. With that achieved, he had been equally successful in helping Goodnight to prove that it would be possible to take herds of cattle to the railroad in Kansas.*

Having proven himself to be a first-class cowhand, Dusty went on to be acknowledged as a very capable trail boss, round-up captain, and a town-taming lawman. In a contest at the Cochise County Fair, he won the title of the Fastest Gun In the West, by beating many other exponents of the pistolero arts.

Dusty Fog never found his lack of stature an impediment. In addition to being naturally strong, he had taught himself to be completely ambidextrous. Possessing fast reflexes, he could draw and fire either, or both, of his Colts with lightning speed and great accuracy. Ole Devil Hardin's valet, Tommy Okasi, was Japanese and from him Dusty had learned ju jitsu and karate. Neither had received much publicity in the Western world, so the knowledge was very useful when he had to fight bare-handed against larger, heavier and stronger men.

APPENDIX 2

With his exceptional good looks and magnificent physical development, Mark Counter presented the kind of appearance that many people expected of Dusty Fog. It was a fact of which they would take advantage when the need arose.

While serving as a lieutenant in General Bushrod Sheldon's cavalry regiment, Mark's merits as an efficient and courageous officer had been overshadowed by his taste in uniforms. Always a dandy, coming from a wealthy family had allowed him to indulge in his whims. His clothing, particularly a skirtless tunic, had been much copied by the other young bloods in the Confederate States' Army, despite considerable opposition and disapproval on the part of hidebound senior officers.

When peace had come, Mark followed Sheldon to fight for Emperor Maximilian in Mexico. There he had met Dusty Fog and the Ysabel Kid, helping with the former's mission. On returning to Texas, Mark had been invited to join the OD Connected's floating outfit. Knowing that his elder brothers were sufficient to help his father, Big Rance Counter, run the R Over C Ranch in the Big Bend country—and suspecting that life *would be more exciting with Dusty and the Kid—he had accepted.*

An expert cowhand, Mark was known as Dusty Fog's right bower, and gained acclaim by virtue of his enormous strength and ability in a roughhouse brawl. However, due to his being so much in the small Texan's company, his full potential as a gunfighter received little attention. Men who were in a position to know stated that he was second only to the Rio Hondo wizard in speed and accuracy.

Many women found Mark's appearance irresistible, including Miss Martha Jane Canary, who was better known as Calamity Jane. Only one held his heart, the lady outlaw Belle Starr. It was several years after her death that he courted and married Dawn Sutherland, who he had met on the Goodnight trail drive to Fort Sumner.

APPENDIX 3

The only daughter of Long Walker, war leader of the Pehnane—
*Wasp, Quick Stinger, or Raider—Comanche Dog Soldier lodge
and his French Creole pairaivo[1] married an Irish Kentuckian
adventurer called Sam Ysabel but died giving birth to their first
child. Given the name Loncey Dalton Ysabel, the boy was raised
in the fashion of the* Nemunuh.[2] *With his father away much of
the time on the family business of first mustanging, then smuggling, his education had been left to his maternal grandfather.[3]
From Long Walker, he had learned all those things a Comanche
warrior must know: how to ride the wildest freshly caught mus-
tang, or when raiding—a polite name for the favorite* Nemenuh
*sport of horse stealing—to subjugate a domesticated mount to his
will; to follow the faintest of tracks and conceal traces of his own
passing; to locate hidden enemies yet remain concealed himself
when the need arose; to move in silence through the thickest of
cover or on the darkest of nights; and to be highly proficient in*

[1] *Pairaivo:* "first or favorite, wife."
[2] *Nemunuh:* "The People," the Comanche Indians' name for their nation.
[3] Told in *Comanche.*

the use of a variety of weapons. In all these subjects the boy had proved an excellent pupil. He had inherited his father's rifle-shooting skill and, while not real fast on the draw—taking slightly over a second, where a tophand would come close to half of that time—he could perform adequately with his colt Second Model Dragoon revolver. His excellent handling of one as a weapon had gained him the man-name Cuchilo, "the Knife" among the Pehnane.

Joining his father on smuggling trips along the Rio Grande, he had become known to the Mexicans of the border country as Cabrito, which had come from hearing white men referring to him as the Ysabel Kid. Smuggling did not attract mild-mannered, gentle-natured pacifists, but even the toughest and roughest men on the bloody border had learned that it did not pay to tangle with Sam Ysabel's son. His education and upbringing had not been such that he was possessed of an overinflated sense of the sanctity of human life. When crossed, he dealt with the situation like a Pehnane Dog Soldier—to which lodge of savage, efficient warriors he belonged—swiftly and in a deadly effective manner.

During the war the Kid and his father had begun by riding as scouts for the Gray Ghost, John Singleton Mosby. Later their specialized talents had been used by having them collect and deliver to the Confederate States' authorities in Texas supplies that had been run through the U.S. Navy's blockages into Matamoros or purchased elsewhere in Mexico. It had been hard, dangerous work and never more so than on the two occasions when they had been involved in missions with Belle Boyd.[4]

Sam Ysabel had been murdered soon after the end of the war. While hunting for the killers, the Kid had met Dusty Fog and, later, Mark Counter. Engaged on a mission of international importance, Dusty had been very grateful for the Kid's assistance. When it had been brought to a successful conclusion, learning that the Kid no longer wished to continue a career of smuggling, Dusty had offered him work at the OD Connected Ranch. When

[4] Told in *The Bloody Border* and *Back to the Bloody Border*.

the Kid had stated that he knew little about being a cowhand, he had been told that it was his skill as a scout that would be required. His talents in that line had been most useful to the floating outfit.

In fact the Kid's acceptance had been of great benefit all round. Dusty had gained a loyal friend, ready to stick by him through any danger. The ranch had obtained the services of an extremely capable and efficient man. For his part the Kid had been turned from a life of petty crime—with the ever-present danger of having it develop into more serious law breaking—and become a useful member of society. Peace officers and honest citizens might have been thankful for that, as he would have made a terrible and murderous outlaw if he had been driven into such a life.

Obtaining his first repeating rifle while in Mexico with Dusty and Mark, the Kid became acknowledged as a master in its use. In fact at the Cochise County Fair he won the first prize—one of the fabulous Winchester Models of 1873 "One Of A Thousand" rifles—against very stiff competition.[5] Also it was in great part through his efforts that the majority of the Comanche Indian bands agreed to go on to the reservation.[6] Nor could Dusty Fog have cleaned out the outlaw town of Hell without the Kid's assistance.[7]

[5] Told in *Gun Wizard*.
[6] Told in *Sidewinder*.
[7] Told in *Hell in the Palo Duro* and *Go Back to Hell*.

J.T. EDSON

Brings to Life the Fierce and Often Bloody Struggles of the Untamed West

___ THE BAD BUNCH	20764-9	$3.50
___ THE FASTEST GUN IN TEXAS	20818-1	$3.50
___ NO FINGER ON THE TRIGGER	20749-5	$3.50
___ SLIP GUN	20772-X	$3.50
___ TROUBLED RANGE	20773-8	$3.50

THE FLOATING OUTFIT SERIES

___ THE HIDE AND TALLOW MEN	20862-9	$3.50
___ THE NIGHTHAWK	20726-6	$3.50